WARRIOR MAGIC

WARRIOR MAGIC

THE LEIRA CHRONICLES™ BOOK 11

MARTHA CARR

MICHAEL ANDERLE

DISRUPTIVE IMAGINATION

LMBPN Publishing
PMB 196, 2540 South Maryland Pkwy
Las Vegas, NV 89109

Version 1.02, January 2021
eBook ISBN: 978-1-64971-207-3
Print ISBN: 978-1-64971-208-0

From Martha

*To everyone who still believes in magic and all the possibilities
that holds.*

To all the readers who make this entire ride so much fun.

*To Louie, Jackie, and so many wonderful friends who remind me
all the time of what really matters and how wonderful life can be
in any given moment.*

*And finally, a special thank you to John Nelson of the Austin,
Texas Police Department who patiently answers all of my
questions. I hope I made you proud. Thank you for your service.*

From Michael

*To Family, Friends and
Those Who Love
To Read.
May We All Enjoy Grace
To Live The Life We Are
Called.*

CHAPTER ONE

Leira walked up to the entrance of the dignified Hay-Adams hotel as the doorman pulled open one of the large mahogany doors. The grey-haired man was dressed in a long chocolate brown coat and matching pants and gave only a slight nod, not making eye contact. Leira glanced back at the White House, barely visible in the distance just beyond Lafayette Square.

She pulled her leather jacket closer against the biting wind that had popped up that morning and stepped into the lobby. She only went a few feet before she stopped at a round table topped with a vase of large white peonies, running her finger along the marble top.

"Wow. The general has upped his game." She turned in a slow circle, looking up at the ornate mahogany and plaster arches, lit by a line of crystal chandeliers.

"Ms. Berens?" A man in a bespoke dark suit and thin tie waited patiently, his hands folded neatly behind his back.

Leira looked down, aware that several guests were suddenly looking at her. "You're my escort?"

"Yes ma'am. If you would follow me." He walked next to her, leading her past the front desk and by the elevators to the service elevator located down a narrow side hallway. He took out a key and made a quarter turn to the right in the lock as the doors to the elevator slid open. "After you." He held out his arm, a barely noticeable smile.

Leira stepped on, unable to resist letting a little magic flow through her, her eyes glowing. "Wizard. You work for the Feds?"

His smile grew broader as he turned the key in another lock on the panel as the doors closed. "I am an ally at times." Leira saw the intertwined S's on his wrist as he dropped his arm.

The elevator descended three floors, just under the basement, coming to a stop with a slight jerk. The doors opened and a musty, damp smell wafted into the small elevator car. The wizard stepped out first and reached for a flashlight on a nearby shelf, shining a beam straight ahead of them. "We're almost there," he said, turning back to wait for Leira. She stepped out onto a slate floor that quickly changed to large, stone pavers leading down a wide tunnel, held up with oak beams along the sides.

"Where exactly are we?" A rat ran over Leira's foot, disappearing into the darkness. She waved, glancing at her escort, who was arching an eyebrow, the corners of his mouth turned up in a smile. "It's a thing," she said.

"Of course. I've learned not to be surprised." He held the light straight, stepping carefully to avoid any puddles of stale water. "We are in a tunnel that predates the country. It was set up by revolutionary magicals who believed in the new experiment." He turned his head slightly, the same gracious smile. "Democracy was like a new kind of magic. My grandmother loved telling us stories about the part she played. My grandfather helped build this tunnel. It's protected by wards that are centuries old and heavily layered."

"That explains why I couldn't portal."

"Rules forbid any portals within a hundred yards of the hotel. No need to hold up a neon sign for the wrong sort. Dark magic knows of the tunnels' existence but so far they've never gotten hold of a map."

The light shone on a protrusion from the dirt along the top of wall. A Light Elf, outlined as if they were trapped. The wizard saw her alarm and shone the light on another spot. A mound of dirt shaped like a ground hog, curled up and sleeping. "It's a side effect of all the magic that's been layered in these walls for protection. The dirt has been known to take the form of anyone who passes through here. It's creepy, but harmless."

"Perfect for Halloween," said Leira, glancing up at a dirt outline of a Dwarf with its mouth wide open. Leira reached out to touch the dirt but the wizard stopped her with a shake of his head, still smiling.

"My favorite holiday, of course. Here we are."

He placed his hand flat against the wood posts that made up the mud sill. A narrow beam of sparkling blue light shot out, straight into his eyes as he kept them open wide. The bearing wall began to shimmer, reshaping itself into a low door. Once it solidified, the wizard removed his hand and the door swung open on its own. "Watch your head," he said, as he ducked. "Gnomes built most of these and sometimes they like to leave reminders."

Leira bent over and went through the narrow door into another hallway as the wall reshaped itself behind her. "Another precaution," said the wizard. "They're everywhere. Nothing is as it seems down here. Keep that in mind." He waved her over to his side. "You have to be next to me for this one. No one gets past this ward without being screened."

"What does it do?" asked Leira, stepping up next to him. Light streamed over both of them, searching.

"Checks intentions. It's an older ward, but very effective. And God help you if your intentions don't check. You become a neutral threat pretty quickly."

Leira's forehead wrinkled as the wall in front of her tore itself from its moorings, sliding to the right, revealing old tree roots. Silt poured down in the entryway. They waited till it stopped and the wizard tilted his head toward the entrance. "This is where I leave you. I have to get back to my post or I'll be docked. A break can only last so long. Humans," he said, with a smile.

"Thank you." Leira had one foot through the door and turned back. "How do I get back out of here?" But the wizard was already gone.

Standing in front of her in a room with a metal table and two chairs was General Anderson. His hat sat on the table, lined up perfectly in front of a chair. "Leira, I'm glad you could make it."

She stepped through and waited. The loud noise from the earth rumbling to repair itself stopped her from answering right away. "Good morning. This seems a little over the top. I thought the phone line was secure enough for mission details."

The general pressed his lips together. "Normally, yes. But we have a unique problem this time. Have a seat. Go ahead, don't make me ask anything twice." He sat down without waiting for her. Leira took the other seat, sitting on the edge.

"There's an old legend of an artifact that was so powerful it could tear a hole into the world in between," he said, shaking his head with a grim expression. "Have you heard the tale of the Erebus and the Terror? Two ships lost over a hundred years ago in the arctic."

"Someone thought it was a good idea to christen a ship, the Terror."

"Makes you wonder. They were said to be on a secret mission to hide a terrible artifact. One of the oldest on this planet and capable of punching holes in the thin veil between us and the world in between. But the two ships disappeared suddenly, along with most of the crew. Some were found on land by the local Inuit, all dead. At least that's how the story goes. It was covered up and a decision was made to never speak of it again. I think the higher ups were hoping a problem had just tragically solved itself."

"I take it the problem has resurfaced."

"Quite literally. A scientific expedition named Americae Science used robots to uncover the two ships. A human expedition that thought the old stories were myths. Now, they've gone missing as well."

The color drained from Leira's face and she felt a hum along the back of her neck. "How many are missing?"

"Well, from eighteen forty-eight there were over twenty

men from the two ships. More recently, eight. Six men and two women. We suspect the robots brought up the artifact mixed in with other more mundane contrivances."

"What does this artifact look like?"

"It's a mirror in a brass setting with a handle. Stare at it too long and you start to see the other side, clawing toward the mirror." The general shook his head, wearily. "It must have sucked them all in. I can't imagine."

"Is there anyone at the site now?"

The general sliced the air with his arm. "No! It's forbidden. There was an argument to leave it wherever it's laying but other humans are bound to trip over it. The families of the expedition are trying to raise money to go and search the area."

"Of course. They're thinking there must be evidence of what happened to them."

"We need you to leave right away. There's equipment waiting for you at an old abandoned whaling post that's not far from where the ships are located. I will send you the coordinates as soon as I'm out from under all these wards." General Anderson lowered his chin, staring at Leira. "Do not look into the mirror, for any reason. You'll find artifact bags among the supplies we have provided. Use one quickly and seal it shut. Lois will be waiting for the artifact once it's secure. The coordinates for that will be sent as well."

"There's more to this story, isn't there? Otherwise, you could send your own team for a mere retrieval. There's a lot of Special Ops who could get this done."

General Anderson spread his hands on the table, hesitating, but only for a moment. "Something strange is happening there that's affected the wildlife. In particular the aquatic wildlife. They've morphed into dangerous, aggressive creatures."

Leira furrowed her brow. "That's a new one. I've never heard of the world in between emitting anything that could scramble DNA."

"Hard to say where it's coming from, but it's there. It's what attracted the scientists. They were convinced it was from nuclear waste. I'd consider it except for the reports from the locals about the powers of an ordinary fish."

"Another artifact may be leaking magic. A secondary mission that was never recorded anywhere." Leira stood.

"I suspect the same." General Anderson stood and put out his hand. "Be careful, my friend."

A shiver went down Leira's back as she shook his hand. "You've never done that before and we've taken some pretty hairy rides. Don't count me out. I'll be back before you know it and we'll have sushi. On you."

The general chuckled, the strain still showing on his face. "Deal. You can go back the way you came to leave here. You'll find the entrances open along the path you've already taken."

"There's a lot more to this place, though," said Leira, looking around at the simple room.

"Much more, but that is another secret that will only be revealed when it's needed. Remember what I said. Put the mirror away immediately and get out of there as fast as you can. The bounty will be double your normal fee."

"You know it's bad when the Feds will double the pay." Leira rubbed her hands together. "I do have my eye on a large refrigerator." She walked toward the wall where she entered as it began to tear itself apart, creating an exit. "I'll see you soon," she said, without turning around, "I give you my word." She stepped through to the tunnel and got moving. "The sooner this one is done, the better," she muttered.

CHAPTER TWO

Leira hugged Correk tight around his neck. "We said there would be no secrets. This one is gonna be hairy."

"You want me to tag along? We could bring the troll and make it a family trip."

"We take strange road trips," said Leira, heading for the hall closet. She dug around in the back till she found the old puffy coat Mara had given her for DC winters. "This will have to do till I get to the outpost and can change." She saw Correk's worried expression, his arms crossed over his chest. She put her hands on his arms. "We knew that when I took the job as a bounty hunter hairy shit was gonna come up. This isn't the last time something dark and desperate will need my attention. Or yours for that matter."

He loosened his arms and she burrowed her way between them, wrapping her arms around him and resting her head on his chest. "I will take every precaution and with some luck, will be home by dinner. Have the hot coffee waiting. You know, without Hagan, I drink a lot less of the stuff." She looked up at Correk, their noses touching. "I may have to change that. Mmmm coffee."

He lowered his head far enough to kiss her, lingering. "Come home to me."

"If it's the last good thing I do."

He kissed her again before she slipped into the coat and stepped back, opening a portal. "I left the coordinates on the kitchen table. Only intervene if you sense I'm leaving this world," she said, as the portal opened and an icy blast of cold air whistled through the hallway of the house, blowing back Correk's long hair. She slipped on a pair of sunglasses against the glare, the cold easily cutting through her coat.

Correk didn't move, giving her a thumbs up as the portal grew smaller. She watched him for as long as she could till the portal closed, the sparks fizzing along the cold, packed snow.

"Time to get inside." She held her arm up against the wind and made her way toward the old metal building. "Cowboy boots were not made for this kind of cold." The door opened with a loud creak and she stepped inside, pushing the door closed. It was warmer, but not by much.

Laid out on a table was a snow suit with a fur-lined hood and proper boots and gloves, along with goggles. An iPad was lying next to everything with a post-it note that say, 'pick me up'. Leira touched it with her right hand and it activated, displaying a virtual screen in the air. Images of the underwater wreck and the scientist's camp scrolled through the air. In the camp photos, a journal was left open with a pen sitting nearby. A plate with a half-eaten sandwich was at the other end. Leira scrolled back to the photos of the wreck at the decaying wood, still somewhat preserved by the frozen waters. Barely noticeable in the background was claw marks, dug into the side of a door frame. She quickly waved her hand, going back to the photo of the camp. "There it is," she whispered. "Claw marks in the table. Enough time to know what was happening, but not enough to do much about it. That is useful information."

The door opened at the far end of the room and a tall, muscular man with a thick mop of black hair came in, wearing the same kind of polar jumpsuit. "Not if you follow the tenets of your mission." He tapped an ear. "Wolf hearing. It picks up everything."

"You're a shifter."

"Well, most people call me, Jack. I'm your helpful magical on this mission."

"General Anderson didn't mention anyone else being here. In fact, he said this was too dangerous to bring anyone else along."

"I'm not his idea. Lois saw things differently and since I live in the area." He held out his arms to the sides. "I'm an arctic shifter. A native to the area in human form. It translated to my wolf form too." He went through her supplies, checking them. "You're going to need me. Lois was right. Make sure you take a few of these energy goo packets in case we're stranded, or worse," he said, with a shrug. "Could come in handy."

"If we're sucked into..."

"The world in between? Not that kind of worse. Then it's mission over. If we get stuck at the camp site. The flares from the sun sometimes mess with magic out here. That's why they have you opening a portal to this fine establishment."

Leira looked around at the rust dripping down a wall and the frost building up on the one window. "I'm going there now. I have dinner plans. Are you ready?"

"I stay ready. Easier that way out here. Don't look at me like that. This is harsh terrain. It doesn't forgive much." He turned his back to her. "Hurry up and change and we can get moving. We'll have to travel by ATV's to get there. This is far enough away to use a portal but it's the only safe zone." He glanced over his shoulder. "You were the one who said you wanted to get home by dinner. Better get a move on."

Leira arched an eyebrow, peeling off her coat and boots.

"Lose those jeans. That's a newbie move. If they get wet, they're worse than if you never have them on at all. Use the long johns instead. They're fleece lined. Trust me, you're gonna thank me," he said, his hands on his hips.

She unzipped her pants and left them on the bench, pulling on the oatmeal-colored long johns. Next came her long-sleeved shirt, but underneath was an old A Team t-shirt, a present from the troll the last Christmas. She pulled the long johns up over it and buttoned them up to the top. The snow suit was roomy and slid on easily, along with a fresh pair of socks and the boots. "You can turn around now," she said, pulling on the laces till they were tied tight. She picked up a handful of the energy goo packets and stuffed them in her pocket.

"You're gonna need more than that if things go sour."

"Then let's not let them go that sour." Leira slid the

backpack on, adjusting the straps and put the goggle around her neck, slipping on the wool knit hat.

"You ever work an ATV before?"

"First time, but that's kind of been my life for the past year. I've ridden a motorcycle before, though."

"You'll be a natural," said Jack, smiling, windburn on his cheeks. "We're off to see the wizard," he said, opening the door, letting the cold wind blow into the building. "Magical joke."

Leira put the goggles on her face, adjusting them and slipped on the gloves. "Yeah, I've never heard that one before."

The pair pushed outside and around to the back of the building where two Kenda Bearclaw ATVs sat side by side. Jack pointed to the one on the left and waited for Leira to get on board. "The controls are pretty self-explanatory." He pointed to the pegs near the bottom. "Keep your feet on those at all times. Never let a foot drag. Ever. Don't lock your elbows and try to relax in the seat." He turned his face away from the wind. "There's a clutch lever on the left side of the handlebars and a brake lever on the right. Keep a couple fingers around them, ready to go at any moment. Turning is different from a bike. It's more like a car. If we have to make a hard turn, lean in the other direction. You want all the wheels to keep contact with the ground. You think you have it?" He shook his head. "You must be some kind of badass to send you out here to this place at a moment's notice."

"I get the job done." Leira was yelling over the wind.

"Fair enough," yelled Jack. Follow me just to one side so you don't get the blowback, but no further away than that.

There can be sudden crevices that are hundreds of feet deep. That would not be a good ending to this caper." He smiled and gave her a two finger wave as he got on his ATV and started it up, not wasting any time.

Leira pulled in energy, her eyes glowing behind her goggles, and set an intention. "You're at the helm, now," she whispered, her lips already growing stiff.

They rode along a path that was already packed down with an occasional snow drift blowing across it. Jack approached a tall hump of snow, pulling to the right at the last minute and leaning to the left. Leira felt her magic encircle the ATV, helping her adjust.

By the time they reached the camp, her cheeks were frozen, but they had arrived without incident. *A good omen.*

The magic was still pulsing through her, despite what Jack had said, and the scar on her belly was burning under her clothes. *Something's up.*

Jack parked his ATV and got off, waiting for Leira. They entered the shelter made of a metal frame, covered in a heavy tan material. It had the shape of an oversized brown igloo in the middle of a white frozen desert.

Leira stomped her feet at the door, imitating Jack and pulled off her gloves, the symbols creeping up the back of her hands, flipping over and over.

Jack's eyebrows went up, watching the patterns and looking up at Leira with a wide-eyed respect. "You're still connected to your magic. That's a first. Don't count on it, though. It could break off at an inopportune moment."

Leira went to put her gloves on the table and felt her stomach lurch. She pressed the back of her hand against her mouth as a stench filled her nose. "Don't you smell that?" She pressed a hand against the table to steady herself and swallowed hard. Magic crawled up her spine, swirling in her head, making it harder to think clearly. "There's something very powerful nearby."

Jack turned around, looking at the cupboards and the metal lockers and started opening the cabinets closest to him. Leira gritted her teeth and lunged for him, pulling him back. "No! Whatever it is, it's giving off waves of energy. We don't know a fucking thing about it." She pushed Jack behind her and pulled off her backpack, trying to get her fingers to work faster. "Frozen fish sticks for fingers," she muttered, digging through the side pocket. Inside was a black silicone bag laced through with bronze threads provided by the Silver Griffins. Leira slid it open and held it out in front of her, using her body as a Geiger counter. "It's not the cupboard."

She stepped closer to the lockers and her eyes began to sting. "I'm getting warmer. The bitch is close." She started to reach for the metal handle on the locker but could feel the powerful hum and pulled back, hesitating.

"Here!" Jack threw her a glove. "See if this helps. Maybe it'll work like an oven mitten."

Leira shook her head, pressing her eyes shut for a moment against the nausea, but put the glove on anyway. "One, two... three!" She fell forward, grasping the handle tight. Her arm shook violently, making her head bob and her shoulder ache from the effort. She wrenched open the door releasing a purple blast of light that lifted her off her feet, throwing her backward, into Jack.

They rolled, feet over head on the ground, coming to a stop at the far wall. Leira forced herself onto her knees, throwing up in a nearby olive green metal trash can. She wiped her face on her sleeve and reached out for the edge of the table, lifting herself to her feet.

"You okay?" She looked back at Jack and saw the line of thick grey and white fur appearing along the back of his neck. "Fuck this. Something is throwing off magic. Trust. Trust in my own powers," she said through clenched teeth. She curled her hands into fists, one still in a glove and lowered her shoulders, pushing forward. The bag was laying on the ground near the locker. She scooped it up and kept her knees bent, looking inside the locker. A confused look came over her face. "What the hell?"

In front of Leira was a stack of cans with faded labels that all said beans. She reached out with her gloved hand and picked up a dented can. The containment bag ready in her other hand. The smell of rot instantly grew stronger. "I think I found the problem. Son of a..." The glove was smoking, the outer layer slowly melting.

Leira's head rocked back, her eyes rolling backward and the scar on her belly warming. Images of men with long, scruffy beards appeared in her head, along with the main sail of a tall ship. The men were clustered together, admiring a mirror and patting each other on the back.

They broke with the mission.

The images kept unfurling in her mind. They hushed each other, looking around at the crew and followed in a line down wooden stairs into a narrow galley. An older man with lined, ruddy skin pulled the mirror back out and this time held it up higher to see his own reflection, the others gathered around him.

The mirror glowed in a soothing warm light, drawing them in closer. Their eyes were wide with curiosity.

But the jubilant expressions were quickly turning to concern, and then to horror.

Leira could feel each emotion roiling through her, temporarily connecting her to the moment in time.

Faces were appearing on the other side of the looking glass, pushing themselves against the divide till there was a tear.

Hands reached through, clawing at each other, reaching for the men who stared, dumbfounded and entranced. The mirror was fused to the man's hand and his eyes had gone blank.

Leira felt a pounding in her head, wanting to reach back through time and yell at them to drop the mirror, but she knew it was hopeless.

There was a flash of light, followed by a grey billowing shadow that rolled around the room. Leira could hear the screams and saw a calloused hand with a faded tattoo emerge from the clouds, clawing at a door frame. The hand slipped off the door frame and swatted the air, looking for something else. The outstretched fingers found an unopened can of beans and pulled it back into the morass. It reemerged, empty and covered in scratches, searching for something else.

Leira felt a familiar and powerful tug. The same one she had encountered every time the dark mist had sought her out.

Sloop!

The hand was pulled back into the cloud and the shadows swirled in a tightening horizontal formation, pulling back into the mirror in a funnel-shaped dense mist. At the last moment, the can of beans appeared in the air, dropping to the ground. Crew members came piling into the galley, answering the screams and pleading but found nothing. A wiry man with only a few teeth left in his mouth, picked up the stray can and yelped. He tried to drop it, roaring with anger, but couldn't. It was burning his flesh, the fire creeping up his arm, quickly turning his entire body to ash. The others backed up toward the stairs, running away as the last of the ashes scattered along the floor.

Leira gulped in air, the memories fading. The can had almost burned through the glove.

"There's no time for the bag. Open the fucking door!"

Jack crawled half on his knees, half standing to the door, pushing it open and holding it there. Leira leaned back, her arm in the air. She let go of any resistance within and let her magic surround her.

"Now!" yelled Jack. His hands were already lengthening, claws appearing.

Leira pitched the can as hard as she could, her magic fighting to wrap itself around the relic. The glove slid off her hand, fused with the can as her magic helped to push it through the air. The menace sailed out the door, hitting a snowbank and instantly melting its way down through the ice with a loud sizzle. "That's gonna leave a mark. I think I get why the ocean life around here is on the weird side," Leira yelled over the sound of the wind. The nausea rolled over her one last time, lessening with every second. Jack reached out for the door handle, blinking at the biting wind. He pulled the door shut, locking it and slumped to the ground. "How the fuck did you know it was that can?"

Leira looked back at the stack. "The only one that didn't have any dust on it. The vibrations kept anything from sticking."

"You guessed? You should have used the containment bag to pick it up."

"I deduced. You have a point, but then I wouldn't know what happened. I saw everything. It was a horror show of images rolling through my brain."

Jack laid flat on the floor, his body changing back and the fur disappearing. "How the hell did you do that? Even my kind can't do that."

Leira looked at the rosy color of her palm and went and knelt by Jack. "What exactly is your kind?" Her eyes glowed as she helped him up. "I can see you're a magical, but not anything I've seen before. You're a combination of a shifter and... and something else." Her fingers trailed the claw marks in the table. "The mirror must be nearby," she muttered.

"An arctic witch. We keep to ourselves." He staggered on his feet and sat down hard on a metal chair. "You didn't answer my question. What are you?"

Leira opened the containment bag still in her other hand. "Mostly a Jasper Elf." Her eyes kept glowing as a ribbon of her energy made its way around the room, searching for other sources of magic. The magic sputtered and sparked, creating painful jabs in Leira's head. She clamped her hands on either side of her skull, determined not to pull back.

"I've heard of your kind. My auntie talked about a male

Jasper Elf who rescued her once a long time ago. He was training to be a Fixer."

Leira breathed in deeply, letting it out as the magic stabilized. "You're about to have a small world moment. Jackson. That must have been Jackson, my father. Focus, Jack. The real bogeyman is still in here with us. We can't afford to come up on it accidentally. Have you ever seen a tear in the world in between?"

"Only legends. That was enough." He sniffed the air. "Don't throw me shade. Shifters can smell magical trails."

"The place has tried to invite me in a few times. It's worse than the idea of dying."

Jack put the back of his hand over his nose. "Something old and dark that way there," he said, pointing to a pale blue and white pouch half hidden under the cabinets. On the top was printed '*Americae Science Expedition*'.

"Winner winner, chicken dinner." Leira crouched by the pouch and glanced up at the surroundings. "Nothing in here seems to have gotten the same treatment as that can of beans." Leira bit her lower lip, looking at the bag from different angles. "What do you say? One of us holds the containment bag open and the other opens the bag and lets the mirror slide out. Let gravity do the rest. Which bag do you want?"

"I'll take the containment bag." Jack swallowed hard and pulled himself to his feet. "Let's get this over with. There is actual fur standing up on the back of my neck. I don't like this job at all."

Leira narrowed her eyes, pursing her lips. "We may only have a second. Make sure the bag is as wide as you can hold it and turn your head away. Understand? Close it without ever looking at the bag."

"Solid plan. Let's go. You want to be back in time for dinner, right?"

"I want to be anywhere but here, frankly." Leira waited till Jack was in position. "Let's put the bobackslappyass on this bitch." She glanced up at him with a crooked smile. "An old Texas friend of mine with fiery red hair likes to say that." She slowly lifted the bag, holding it by the edges and got it into place over the silicone containment. "One, two, three." She tipped it over as the mirror slid out, facing her.

It quickly fell into the containment pouch, but not before Leira saw the face of the old sailor looking back at her, shaking his head. His mouth was forming a word. *Run.*

The mirror had twinkled at an edge, drawing Leira closer. The darkness had tried to open and take her inside. She felt a shiver go down her spine as Jack closed the bag. He held it out in front of him, bent over, taking in deep breaths.

"Let me take that." Leira carefully stowed the bag in her backpack and put the remaining glove back on her hand. "Let's get the fuck out of here."

"Agreed. Here. You wear my glove."

"I'll be fine. You need it too."

"Don't be stubborn. I'm a local and my skin is fur-lined on the inside. Go on, take the help. We need you to get back in one piece and deliver that doorway to hell to its final resting place." He adjusted the goggles on his face. "Imagine the dark evil that created that shit. Hopefully, they're dead and gone."

"Tell everyone you know to maybe leave local seafood off their plate."

"We already knew something was up. My entire village is made up of shifters. Some are fox and bear shifters. We saw the poisoned energy inside the fish. I'm on a strict frozen pizza regimen."

"Not sure that's any better." Leira slid her hand into the borrowed glove. "Okay, ready."

Jack opened the door and they made their ways to the ATVs. Leira waited for Jack to leave first, following his trail just to the side as instructed. A thought kept her company the entire way back to the old whaling station. *What if they kept a record?*

CHAPTER THREE

Lois waited for Leira in the study at Turner Underwood's estate. "I thought this would be better," said Lois, pursing her lips. The black patent leather purse dangled from her wrist.

Leira's eyebrows went up as she pulled out the containment bag. "Better than Silver Griffins headquarters. You must have an inside problem." She held the bag out, memories of the nausea washing over her. "Here you go. Bury this beauty somewhere good and deep where no one will even remember it exists."

Lois took the bag and laid it on Turner's heavy, ornate wood desk. "That would be a foolish mistake, my dear. If we forget, it leaves an opening for the curious to come digging around what doesn't belong to them. If we remember, we keep up our wards. It's the only way. Never wish to forget. It's a very dangerous path."

Leira stifled a tired yawn, covering her mouth. "This one really beat the shit out of me. Feels like tiny fists were punching me from the inside. Are you good from here or do you need an escort to the vault? I suppose that could attract attention. I don't suppose the vault is in Turner's house," she said with a laugh, watching Lois.

"I'm good from here. Patsy is here with me. She's busy rummaging through Turner's pantry but once her pockets are filled, she'll come back, and we can catalog the item."

"What's the label gonna read? Doorway to hell?"

"Something along those lines."

Leira lifted her hands, her body aching and created a ball of light in her hands, pulling at the sides till the portal opened to her bedroom on the third floor. "I don't even want to bother with stairs," she muttered, climbing through to the creaking wood floor. The troll bounced into view, climbing up her leg, hanging off a pants pocket and waving at Lois.

Lois smiled wearily and waved as the portal closed, the sparks flittering around her sensible shoes. "Patsy?" she yelled, walking to the study door and leaning out into the hallway. "Surely, you've foraged enough already."

Patsy poked her head out of a doorway further down the hall. There was a smudge of chocolate frosting on her cheek. "I've only half started," she said, in wonder. "It's amazing. He has treats I've never even heard of. Will you look at that?" she shouted. "There's Abba Zaba bars! I haven't seen those for a hundred years. Do they still make them?"

"Yes, bring me one of those. But leave a few things for Turner."

"I've been sampling different things trying to find some new favorites. Are we in a hurry?"

"Are we in a hurry?" Lois pressed her lips together, her hands on her hips. "We're on the tail end of a mission," she barked. "There's a hairy beast of an artifact waiting for us to shove it someplace dark before anyone else gets hurt. Get a move on already," she said, waving her arm in frustration.

"Well, when you put it like that..." Patsy trotted down the hallway, the pockets of her long sweater bulging with Ding Dongs poking out the top. "Did I miss Leira? Where'd she go?"

"For Pete's sake, she's already come and gone." She swatted at an offered oatmeal pie. "No, I don't want that. Earle is making a roast tonight. I've been looking forward to it all day." Lois set the purse on the floor and snapped it open. She pulled at the sides, stretching it till the opening was large enough to enter.

Patsy gave a low whistle, looking over the sides of the purse. "That is still one of the coolest things I've ever seen." She pulled the Ding Dongs out of her pocket and opened the plastic wrap, chomping down on the end of one, letting out a satisfied hum.

Lois scooped up the silicone bag, checking the closure and stepped over the sides, onto the stairs. "Stay close and don't drop any crumbs. We don't want anything down here smelling the food and breaking loose."

Patsy wet a finger and pressed it against the crumbs on the front of her shirt, licking them off her finger. "I know you better than that. There's not a chance you didn't lock everything down the second you took office." Patsy lifted the rest of the ding dongs to her mouth as she came down the steps, careful not to spill anything. Lois looked back at her and smiled. Patsy let out a muffled laugh.

"Patsy, I swear, you are the only person I know of that I can have a laugh with while carrying a deadly artifact. You're my work mate, you know that."

"Well, duh. It's a little insulting you have to point it out. I'd zing you for it, but you're carrying that thing."

They got to the bottom of the stairs and the reflecting pool. Patsy wiped off her face and stepped forward. "Let me take this part." She leaned over the side and waited for her reflection to appear. "Patsy Warner, Silver Griffin number two and a half," she said, before the water was completely still. The water slowly reversed itself, flowing counter-clockwise and illuminating Patsy's face. It changed into a deep sea green and reversed direction again, giving its approval.

The far wall began to split apart with a sound like rushing sand, leaving a space just wide enough for the two older witches to march through to the iron balcony. "I've always loved this view," said Lois. She held the containment bag gently against her chest and placed her other hand on the glass opaque ball to the left. "Do it exactly the way I told you," said Lois, nodding.

Patsy stepped up confidently, her pockets rustling. A Zagnut bar slid out, hitting the floor. "Don't worry, I'll get it in a second." She put her hand firmly on the ball on the left.

The virtual dashboard appeared between them. "Silver Griffin number two and a half, Patsy Warner."

"Silver Griffin, number one, Lois Fowler." Her voice

broke, remembering Lacey. "Mirror artifact that can open the world in between." They kept their hands firmly on the glass balls while the dashboard spun until it blurred. It went spinning over the inventory until it came to the end of the line and then blinked, turning itself off without a recommendation.

"Is it broken?" whispered Patsy, leaning down to pick up the candy bar.

"No, and it can't hear you. It *is* a magical vault, but still no ears. I knew where it would point us. This was just a formality," said Lois, removing her hand. She strode over to the metal door, placing her hand firmly against it and waited for the spell to recognize her. The air shimmered around the door and there was a click as Lois pressed harder, opening the door. "Come on, we have a hike ahead of us. We're going into the darkest part of this vault that no one knows about except the head of the Silver Griffins."

Patsy's eyes widened and she finally finished off the Ding Dong. "You trust me that much. I'm honored," she said, licking cream off her lip. She followed Lois out the door, the doorway scanning her body, pausing over her pockets. "You don't suppose it'll hurt the Zagnut, do you?"

Lois rolled her eyes, waiting by the railing.

The cooler air from the reverse air flow chilled Patsy's skin as she stepped up to the railing, rooting around in her pockets. "Where's that Good 'N Plenty."

"Focus, Patsy. That sugar is going straight to your brain today. We need to do this part together."

"Right! Sorry." They each put their hands firmly on the metal railing as it warmed against their skin. Their hands took on a blue glow as Patsy opened her mouth to say something, but Lois shushed her. "I swear Patsy, if you make this thing reject us, I will zing you so hard you won't sit for a month of Sundays and I'll fry every snack in your pockets."

"Geez. You go from a big compliment to threats," she muttered, before pressing her lips together while Lois gave her a sidelong glance.

The stairs responded with a loud creak, moving from the center of the railing over to where the best friends stood side by side. The railing in their hands vanished and Lois started down the stairs. Patsy first checked her pockets, breathing a sigh of relief. "It's kind of nice in here. Too bad you can't decorate. I suppose that would be a little much. You'd have to drag everything into the purse. People would wonder why stuff went in your office but never came out..."

"Patty, this place is perfectly safe. Nothing bad can happen to you down here."

Patty looked taken aback. "I already know that. It's what you're not talking about that has my nerves jumping. I mean, you insist we hike on over to Turner Underwood's digs, which frankly I am on board for all the time, and then you pretty much swear Leira to secrecy that this thing ever existed." Patty pointed a finger. "You think there's a rat in the Silver Griffins," she whispered, fishing through her pockets.

"This is why you're my number two and a half. You put things together quickly." She got to the bottom of the stairs and headed for the middle aisle. Patsy was doing her best to keep up and find something else to sample from her pocket. Lois walked by the fountain pen that belonged to Lucretia Borgia and past the trombone that was found in Arkansas. It turned more than one musician into a legend. But all of them were said to have become obsessed and played till they dropped.

A velvet bag stirred as Patsy went by making her flinch. She stopped to read the card. "Pocketknife of Peter Kurten. Vampire of Dusseldorf." She wrinkled her nose. "Was he really a vampire?" she called out to Lois' retreating back.

"Just a wannabe mad Light Elf and murderer. Sirius should love getting to know him. They're both in Trevilsom."

Patsy whistled, trotting to catch up to Lois who was walking down the aisle that lit up as she passed, quickly dimming again moments later. "This place is endless," said Patsy, a little out of breath. She pulled a tissue out of her sleeve and wiped her forehead. "You could use a golf cart."

Lois shrugged. "Not a bad idea. This place only gets bigger. That's a good one, Two and a Half. Maybe something with pink leather."

"And lights around the top."

The two giggled, elbowing each other as Lois pushed her glasses back up her nose. "Earle would have a fit if he knew the vault got a golf cart before he did. He's been dying to get one to ride around the neighborhood. I keep pointing out that we own a perfectly good Subaru. Those things will go anywhere."

Patsy nudged Lois, pointing at claw marks dug into the metal framing. "That is intense."

"Occasionally... rarely... hardly ever, something puts up

a fight when we're trying to neutralize it forever," said Lois, not slowing down.

"What about today's deposit?"

"Not a chance. It's a special delivery. It's going to stay in the containment bag and go into another bag and then into a specially prepared box in a special room, covered in extra wards."

"Seems dramatic."

"Hardly. I don't know that I've ever heard of a worse artifact, much less had to protect it."

They walked for another mile, the lights coming on and going off as they passed row after row. Finally, they came to what looked like the back wall. The balcony was far in the distance, a pale light barely visible.

Patsy looked to the left and right for some sign of an entrance as Lois took her by the hand. Without a question, she followed her oldest friend and they walked through the wall, appearing on the other side. "I felt that last scanner," said Patsy. "A real tickler."

"Turns into a heat laser if you're a trespasser. You would have instantly become part of the plaster."

Patsy shuddered all over. "Grim, but efficient. Nothing to clean up and a thief helps reinforce the wall." She put her hands on her hips and took a look around at large square room that was dimly lit. On each wall were metal lockers. Some were tall and narrow, and others square and stacked, one on top of the other. There were no locks on any of them, but there were also no handles. Only one was glowing, waiting for the new deposit. Lois went over to it and stood directly in front of it as a number appeared on the metal, along with a new placard. *'Hand Mirror. Useful for Tearing Open the World in Between'.*

"Certainly accurate," said Lois, adjusting her cat-eye pink glasses. One of her favorite pairs. She put out her hand as a brass lever appeared and she pressed down, standing on her toes to use her weight. The lever gave way, letting go with a thud and the metal door swung open. Lois reached in and pulled out a purple velvet bag, sliding in the silicone one and pulling the drawstrings tight. She lifted the lid of a wooden container sitting deeper in the deposit box and carefully laid the bag inside, pressing the box closed, tapping twice. Sparks flew around the opening of the container, sealing as it burned and covering every angle.

Lois wasted no time shutting the metal door and using two hands to lift the brass lever back in place. It slid into place with another solid thud before vanishing, along with the placard and number.

"Seems anticlimactic." Patsy looked around at all the different metal doors.

"That's the point of this special vault. There should be no drama."

"You mentioned something about special wards."

Lois took Patsy's hand and they walked straight at the wall. They popped out the other side. "If anything ever gets out of its containment, the walls will fight back."

"Ghost mercenaries, I like it."

"More like blow up." She puffed out her cheeks and threw up her hands. "Kaboom. Annihilation. The vault knows to make sure not even a cinder survives. It will become nothing."

"Become nothing." Patsy stuck out her lower lip. "How is that even possible? No trace at all. I mean, basic witch lessons taught us that energy cannot be created or destroyed. Everything is always in a constant flux of transformation."

"It's complicated and you're right. It all becomes a fine mist of particles that's deposited somewhere else where no one is, or ever will be."

"Wow, think about that one. The mirror that can trap you in the world in between, which is really neither here nor there, can get blown up and left in a place that isn't where no one will ever be. It's like a riddle. Pez?" She held out a purple Pez candy.

Lois took the candy and unrolled it, sticking it in her cheek to dissolve. "I want to make one stop," she said, tugging on Patsy's arm.

"Impulse buying. Let's do it." She followed Lois to the last row and went to the large crank on the side of the stack, winding it to the right to lower the top shelf closer to her. On it was a green metal cylinder six inches across, with slits all around the base. It was sitting on a wooden spindle base. The placard underneath its shelf read, 'Zoetrope. Bird Metamorphosis'. She reached up, pulling it closer to the edge. Patsy positioned herself to catch anything that could slip out. "Got it," said Lois, with a satisfied smile. "It's an old children's toy. A zoetrope. Like an early movie projector or a fancier flip book. Somewhere in between those two."

In the middle of the drum were strips of paper with different pictures of birds gradually taking flight printed from left to right. Lois balanced the zoetrope against her hip and pulled out a colorful strip. "You put the strip for the bird you want around the inside and then spin the base. When you look inside, it looks like the bird is taking flight. Instead, what happens is the magical turns into that bird."

Patsy's eyes widened with excitement. "It doesn't! You know this is on my bucket list!"

"It does, and I know," said Lois, grinning broadly. "We can become birds, for a little while. It only lasts about an hour. We can only fly around down here, and no one can ever know that we were using some of the archived relics."

Patsy ran pinched fingers over her lips. "Zipped!" She clapped her hands with excitement. "I want to be a lark! Or a warbler. Yeah, a warbler! Is that in there?"

Lois pulled out her wand and tapped the side of the closest stack. A seat pushed out from a slot and she rested the zoetrope, removing a strip of paper. "Hold this in your hands and think about the bird. The paper takes care of the rest." Lois laughed, watching Patsy close her eyes and hold the paper to her chest. A round gray and blue warbler appeared on the strip of paper. It took shape sitting on a branch and progressed to spreading its wings until it was in full flight.

"Okay, put it in here. No, I can't handle it. This part has to be all you." Lois stepped back from the zoetrope, holding a piece of paper in her hands.

Patsy gently laid the paper in the inside and glanced up at Lois, expectantly. "Here goes nothing." She started the spindle, making it spin faster and faster. Patsy's mouth opened in surprise and she also began to spin, changing into a small warbler in mid-flight, darting around the archives.

Lois laughed again, holding her paper close and stepped up, removing Patsy's paper and replacing it with her own. She started up the spindle and held still, feeling a rush from her toes to the top of her head. In an instant, a yellow and black sparrow took her place and spread its wings to follow her friend.

They chased each other back and forth, occasionally stopping to perch along the top of a stack, singing loudly, before taking off again. The sparrow chirped noisily, taking off in the direction of the new chamber, banking sharply to the right. The bird stopped on another stack and chirped again, as if it were annoyed until the warbler began to follow.

The yellow and black bird ducked into a small hole, sliding through a duct as the warbler followed, protesting loudly, but both came out the other side into the chamber by the large whale armor display. The two birds headed straight for another duct, sliding down into the edge of the forest. It wasn't long before the small bird was circling trees and resting on branches, with the warbler always nearby.

Overhead, the dragon sailed across the sky, throwing shadows on the ground. The two birds grew quiet, looking up at the large wing-span made of leathery skin and machine parts. They waited till the dragon was nowhere to be seen and took off again, swooping in lazy circles and singing as loud as they could until the hour was up.

The sparrow was the first to land by the exit from the new exhibit, trying to set a good example. The warbler followed reluctantly, making small, loud chirps. It wasn't long before there was a sudden swirl of color that grew vertically in length as the warbler turned back into Patsy. The sparrow followed and Lois appeared, her glasses askew and her bouffant listing to one side. "What a rush!" she gasped, pushing her hair back in place and straightening her glasses. Patsy looked in her pockets at the candy that was still there. "This stuff has been scanned and transformed and gone through walls. I don't know..."

Lois pressed her hand against the door as a thin light pierced her eye and went to the back of her skull, unlocking the door. They started walking back toward where they had left the zoetrope, chattering away. "It was everything I thought it would be and then some," exclaimed Patsy.

"Did you see that barrel roll I did between the two oak trees?"

"I can now say I've flown through a cloud!"

They didn't stop talking till they got to the toy and Lois picked it up, tucking it under her arm.

"Lois. Even I know we can't take things from the archives. What are you doing, girlfriend? I mean, Earle would lose his mind if you let him be a cardinal for an hour, but it's not worth it."

"That's where rank has its privileges. It's not for Earle, but that's not a bad idea. I have an idea about how I might catch a traitor."

"Oh," said Patsy, nodding. "No one would notice a little songbird perched in a tree. Okay, I'll help you."

"I already figured you would."

"I already figured, you figured. Let's get back upstairs. I want to take a second look at Turner's pantry."

"This time I'm coming with you."

"Be prepared to have your mind blown for the second time today. He has everything."

Lois slung her arm around Patsy's shoulders and listened to her list every candy she could think of as they meandered back through the stacks of artifacts toward the metal stairs.

CHAPTER FOUR

Wolfstan Humphrey stood on a platform wearing sunglasses against the glare. "I will still win, one way or the other," he said, quietly. He looked out over the large, rolling field that stretched for two acres, surrounded by woods made denser with magic to keep out nosy neighbors. Powerful wards did the rest.

An unusual army stood in front of him.

Magicals stood in twenty straight rows, twenty-five across, stomping and clawing the ground and sniffing the air. Their limbs and torsos were distorted with electronics and machine parts where there should have been muscles, bones and tendons. Lieutenants were striding between the rows, keeping everyone in line and preventing anyone from taking a bite out of their compatriots. "Back up!" barked a lieutenant, wielding an electrically charged baton. He glanced the soldier's shoulder, barely stunning him, but with enough of a warning to get him to stand back in line. The magical bore a large burn mark across his back, signifying the rending from a bonded creature.

Wolfstan waved vigorously at a tall Wood Elf, his eyes keeping track of the lieutenants. "Lassiter, report!"

Lassiter made his way to the front, climbing the stairs to the stage. "Five hundred enhanced magicals ready for practical operations, sir." He gave a salute; thick, ropey scars visible along the back of his hand.

"Welcome to my Plan B."

Lassiter turned around to look out over the field. "It's an impressive alternate plan. What did your original one have, nukes?"

"My original one is still in play and involves a more long-term strategy and some finesse. It's been having mixed success, but I suppose that's to be expected. These soldiers are my nukes. If all else fails, they can introduce the world to magic with a bang they'll never forget." He smiled, letting out a laugh that was also equal parts satisfied growl.

"Not a Kilomea among them," said Lassiter, looking at the array of Elves, Gnomes, Wizards and Witches.

"They proved to be too unpredictable. Once transformed they attacked anything relentlessly. I admire it, frankly but without some control it can't work. Is the demonstration ready to begin?"

"The pen has been filled with reluctant volunteers. It should be an interesting match. I feel confident our new soldiers will ultimately win, but the others may take a few casualties. We'll be able to collect insightful data from the process."

"Then let it begin. Open the pen and release the troops." Wolfstan felt a rush of anticipation that was greater than anything he'd ever felt before.

Lassiter formed a ball of light in his hand and sang into it, sending it streaking across the sky. It was the signal to all the lieutenants on the ground. They raised their arms in unison and yelled, "Charge!" The soldiers reacted to the training that had been painfully drilled into them and turned as a unit, running across the expanse, looking for the enemy and jostling each other. Minor wounds were encountered in the mass movement, but no one fell back.

At the other end of the large field the ball of light unlocked a gate, swinging it wide and exposing the hundreds of magicals huddled inside the pen. They looked at each other, some with their eyes wide and others resolute and grim. Many were already wielding wands or forming fireballs, ready to fight.

The ground shook as the soldiers grew closer and magicals began pushing to get out of the pen. Very few hung back, trying to stay hidden. It was obvious that would not be a healthy strategy for long.

Wolfstan watched with glee as the two sides met in battle, magicals valiantly waging war with everything at their disposal, but the carnage was quick and nearly complete.

Lassiter watched without turning away, making notes. "It will become more difficult to get magicals to fight the troops. Their absence will be noted already, and someone will figure out where they're going."

"I'm counting on that," whispered Wolfstan. "Then, we will finally have a worthy test."

Correk felt a pain in his chest, pressing his palm flat against his heart. His face contorted and he sat back hard in the kitchen chair. Leira reached out to him, concerned, pressing her hands on either side of his face. The constant stream of every magical was contorting around him, crying out, begging for his help. He gasped for air, determined to stand and open a portal but Leira pushed him back. She could feel the anguish dying out and knew it was too late. Somewhere, someone had already finished their murderous intent.

CHAPTER FIVE

Correk sat on the back porch, his hands resting on his thighs, not moving except for an index finger that was rhythmically tapping his leg. Leira was leaning on the porch railing, waiting for him to say something.

"I have to go and see for myself," he said at last. "I know there's nothing more to be done, but I have to see it. I have to know."

"We felt the wards surrounding the place. It'll be almost impossible to get past them."

"Not for you."

A look of surprise came over Leira. "Very clever, Fixer. I can send my energy out ahead and you can connect to me. We can see it without ever setting foot on the property."

"Then we're agreed. We find out what happened, right now."

"Okay," said Leira, softly, nodding her head. "Frankly, I would have bolted out of here already and fought my way onto the grounds. But that's why you're the Fixer and I'm not." She stood up, stretching her back. "Let's do this thing. Hallway?"

Correk rose, grim faced and followed Leira into the kitchen. There was the sound of something heavy scraping across the floor, followed by the ping, ping, ping of small, hard objects rolling from one side of the troll's room to another.

Leira looked up at the ceiling, her hands on her hips. "I'd like to say he lost his marbles..."

"Because someone had to."

"Yeah, that," she said, shrugging, "but I can feel it in here that it's bigger than that. What could Yumfuck be up to?"

Correk put his arms around Leira, breathing in the scent of her hair. "He'll tell us when he's ready. Maybe it's a present."

Leira squeezed him tight and let go, taking him by the hand. "Some days I think he's not building anything and he's just gaslighting me."

"Now you know how I feel about the snacks."

Leira took a better look at Correk's tired expression. "After this we're going to Costco and buying out the place."

Something that sounded like a hundred loose marbles rolled back across the floor. "Uh oh," could barely be heard coming from his room.

"Did you hear that?" asked Leira, pointing up. "He's baiting me. I know he's baiting me."

Correk managed a smile that didn't quite get to his eyes. "Let's take this delicate operation to our room. It'll be harder to hear what he's doing and you're going to need to focus."

They climbed the stairs, slowing down at the landing.

Shadows were visible from under the door of two small feet running back and forth and suddenly stopping in the middle.

"Just keep moving," said Correk.

"If he gets in real trouble do I turn blue?" Leira reluctantly turned the corner and started up the stairs for their bedroom.

"No, you would feel like your back was on fire." He shook his head, watching her hesitate. "Sorry I said that. He's fine. He's older than you are and he's entertaining himself."

Leira kept moving up the stairs, getting to the top and turning for their bedroom. "He's a teenager in troll years and he's afraid of nothing. First smell of smoke and we're going in there, no matter what."

"Deal, but not till there's smoke," said Correk, following Leira into the bedroom and quietly closing the door. "Despite his thievery, I'm glad he's here. Some days he reminds me that there's still a lot of joy in life for no good reason." His voice broke on the last words. "I wasn't able to help any of them," he whispered.

Leira put her hand on Correk's chest letting her energy flow with his for a moment. "I love you with all my heart and soul. I don't say that often enough, I think."

"You say it in a million different ways all the time. And I love you just a little bit more." He kissed her, lingering for a moment, then resting his forehead against hers.

"You sure you want to do this?" asked Leira.

"I have to see for myself. I won't understand in my bones the size of the monster if I don't see what he can do."

Leira stepped back and gave a small nod. "Then let's go

bear witness for the dead." She took his hand and breathed in deeply, letting the air out slowly. Magic poured in through her feet, crawling up her body and illuminating the symbols along her arms. They turned slowly, each one the name of a dead magical. Correk read them, an ache in his chest and squeezed Leira's hand.

She set a simple intention and let go. *Let us see.* The energy pushed in on her chest making her take smaller breaths and then just as quickly, released its hold and sailed out ahead, pulling her along with it. She swept out over tall pine as the magic broke itself into ribbons, wrapping back around her, holding her tight. The ground was far below and there were mountains surrounded with a blue haze in the background. Leira took in the view, making note of landmarks.

The tree line began to thin on the horizon, giving way to a long valley. She felt the magic grip her tighter as the far edge of the open area became visible. It was a kaleidoscope of color. Torn blue and yellow clothing, splashed with red and bodies lying prone. Light filled Leira's chest as the energy took her closer. Every other thought or concern slipped away from her.

The symbols on her arms continued to slide over, one name after another, as she drew close enough to see faces. Some were twisted in horror while others looked like they were sleeping. A scattered line of bodies stretched in a direction toward the trees and escape, but no one had even gotten close.

Leira heard a loud and angry wail that penetrated the heavy peace bearing down on her. The energy jerked, yanking her around toward the side of the field.

A lone Light Elf in battle gear was still on the field, the front of his body covered in blood. His right arm and left leg were made up of engineered parts and several more were embedded in his chest. He reared back his head and roared again.

His muscled left arm was in the air and the sunlight was reflecting on something shiny in his hand. *It's a knife.*

She felt Correk's energy spinning around hers, trying to intervene with the Elf, help him. But the Jasper energy was too strong, and his energy was left uselessly whirling, watching the events.

The Light Elf lowered the dagger and dug at the cogs and electronics in his chest. His face was contorted in anger and pain with speckles of blood across the bridge of his nose.

One last great bellow and a small motherboard came loose, flipping end over end in the air. The Light Elf's shoulders sagged, and he dropped the knife, falling forward into the dirt. Down his back was a long burn mark.

Leira's energy exploded, spreading a shimmering light over the field. Her magic came to rest over the fallen, blanketing the field.

A dark SUV came careening over the hill and stopped at the edge of the field. Wolfstan Humphrey got out of the back seat, his eyes glowing and his face twisted in rage. He scanned the ground looking for something, his anger growing as he found nothing. He shook his fist in the air as Leira felt her energy recede, and Wolfstan's image grew fainter. It pulled her back till she was standing in her bedroom, still holding on to Correk's hand. The symbols were still slowly flipping along her arms.

There was a mild ringing in her ears and her mouth was dry. "They looked like ordinary people," said Leira, hoarsely. "They never had a chance."

Correk let go of her hand and sat down on the bed, staring at the wall. "I didn't hear their cries when they were taken or when they were tortured. Wolfstan has figured out a way to wall off their magic. That should not be possible."

"You need to see Turner. This is going to take two Fixers at least." She came and sat next to him, leaning against him. "We're going to stop him, and we'll make him pay for all of it."

"I'm not even sure what that would look like."

"A peace he can't imagine and a cooperation he doesn't want."

"And his destruction," said Correk. "A complete and thorough destruction."

Harkin held the screen door open for Lily. She came into the workroom slowly, her mouth hanging open. "You have everything in here! Is that the new Titan 80-300 Cubed? How did you even get one?" she asked, running a hand up the tall apparatus. "It's like the Hubble telescope but to look at organisms," she said in a hushed voice.

"The Gardener has skills that surpass gardening and animal husbandry it would appear." He watched her delight and was surprised to find himself joining in. "I didn't ask how he did it, mostly because he wouldn't have told me anyway. I'm just grateful for his help."

Lily pulled herself away from the oversized microscope and kept walking around the redesigned lab. Harkin watched her walk by the space that had been Peyton's room. The walls had been removed and it was now a work area. Harkin smiled, still feeling a relief spread through his chest.

"What can I do to help? You have all my research already." Lily clapped her hands together. "Did you have something new in mind?"

Harkin shook his head. "Not yet. Until Wolfstan is stopped, we only have one directive. But it's a slightly different one. I was able to help Peyton, but to some degree it was because of that bowl artifact. It's not a good long-range plan. I want to see if we can help others that have been tortured by Wolfstan."

Lily's eyes widened and she grasped her hands in front of her chest. "You're talking about regeneration. That's next level."

"It's what we did for Peyton. We had to remind his brain cells how to grow new, specific ones and give them tasks. Now we need to see if it's possible to combine magic and technology and do it for other areas of the body, without a unique artifact."

"I'm excited, of course, but that could take years." She shrugged, biting her lower lip. "I suppose we should get started."

Harkin smiled, holding up his hands. "Not so fast. I already have a large piece of the puzzle. It's in a ring that I gave to my son for safekeeping when I was sent away... to Trevilsom," he said, looking down at the floor.

"There's no need to feel shame. We all make mistakes. Real character comes through with how we deal with them."

"Even then, mine had some flaws."

"But look at you now. Let go of what isn't happening anymore. It'll just get in the way. That's all advice from my Aunt Lois."

"Wise magical. You know, you're right. I waited a long time for this very day. Let's start with a blank slate."

"If you could design it yourself, what would it look like?"

Harkin let out a deep, belly laugh that brought the pixies flying by the window to see what was happening. "I would want what I already have," he bellowed in delight.

Lily smiled and pulled out her wand, a small scar visible along her wrist. "Then let's begin. How do we get back that ring?"

"We'll need Leira's help to talk to a mermaid."

"Oh, this is going to be fun."

CHAPTER SIX

Leira got off the stop at Columbia Heights and took the stairs up to the platform at the top, following the other commuters. She passed through the wall, into Starbucks and breathed in the smell of chocolate. "Never gets old."

She passed out onto 14th Street and kept walking, taking a right on Newton till she could see the large stain glass windows stretching for the sky in the distance.

Doc Leahy was waiting for her outside on the stairs in front of the three tall, wooden, red front doors. The wizard looked exactly as he described himself. Scruffy aging hippie in an oatmeal colored cable sweater, jeans and hiking boots.

The trail of magic swirling around him was just as she had suspected. A sparkling green with a trace of darkness sprinkled everywhere. Magic in conflict with itself. She walked up to the bottom of the steps, passing by the church sign with the message, *'Tweet others as you would like to be tweeted'*.

MARTHA CARR & MICHAEL ANDERLE

"A church seems like an odd choice," said Leira.

Doc Leahy chuckled and put out his hand. "I heard you were always direct. It's a quality I admire." He shook Leira's hand and she felt it again. The contest to do the right thing or try an easier, faster path. He let go of her hand, the smile hardening a little. "Before you judge me, get to know me," he said, turning to head up the stairs, shoving his hands in his pocket.

Leira bit her bottom lip and followed him into the open middle door, turning right to go down a narrow, spiral metal staircase. They passed several women sitting out in the hall, children running back and forth, squealing with delight as they played a game of tag. They kept walking to a door further down the hall. Doc pulled out a ring of keys and unlocked it, heading in and not waiting for Leira.

She went in and was taken aback by the piles of paper everywhere, surpassed only by the stacks of books. Some of them held an empty coffee cup, or a pair of reading glasses. Doc sat down behind a large yellow pine desk and moved some papers to the side. He picked up a few more revealing a laptop and scooted it to the center, right in front of him.

"This is old school, particularly for a wizard who knows his way around the magical dark web." Leira sat in the one empty chair in front of the desk. "It looks like you created a nest."

He finally smiled again, the wrinkles deepening around his eyes. "Of sorts. I've found that too much time on the internet causes one to lose faith in just about everything, including the internet. I like a record of things I can hold. Proof it ever existed."

Leira sat back, waiting. "You called this meeting."

"Right. I have another assignment for you, but if we're going to keep working together there are things you need to know." He paused, but Leira kept quiet, patiently watching him. Hagan's old rule number one.

Doc shifted in his chair, pulling a sticky note off the seat, giving it a glance and affixing it to a small brass lamp shade. "I know you can see the trace of darkness still left in me. I was at one time a very powerful wizard in the dark families. I was their doctor and knew all their secrets, and even had a few of my own." He glanced out the tall window at the large oak tree hiding most of the view. "I thought I would be there forever, just like my father before me. But certain events changed things." He swallowed hard and looked down at his hands. "A story for another time. Suffice it to say, I abruptly left and went in search of some kind of redemption."

"You became a minister?" Leira's brow was furrowed.

Doc smiled, rubbing his chin. "No, that would be too far a stretch. I am still a doctor but for the homeless who pass through these doors. This entire basement is devoted to feeding and caring for people who have nowhere else to go."

Leira tilted her head. "Admirable, but leaves large holes in your story."

Doc let out a tired sigh. "Yes, it does." He leaned forward, resting his forearms on his laptop. "I quickly found out that it is impossible to completely escape your past. Dark magicals in need of medical care started showing up here, endangering the wellbeing of the popula-tion this church is dedicated to serve. At first, I thought it meant I would need to move on, and quickly. But, creatures that are hurt or sick are vulnerable and often they want to tell me what is worrying them most. A young wizard named Toby passed through these doors looking for his mother. He had quite the story to tell. The dark families were no longer satisfied with bullying their own kind and drinking expensive wine, living over privileged lives. They wanted more, but no one seemed to be paying attention."

"You became a one-man crusader. Is that your redemption?"

"Redemption doesn't happen in a single act, at least not for me. It's something I have to choose daily and be willing to take on whatever task appears in front of me. Toby brought an interesting task to my attention. The dark families are plotting to monopolize magic as the gates open, but you are in their way."

"I'm their enemy number one. I've been told."

"You're a nuisance, but not their focus. Not anymore. There is a new regime guided by a powerful young witch named, Ariana. She is more pragmatic than her elders, and more dangerous. She will work with anyone for a moment who helps her achieve a step toward her goal. Even the very thing she wants to kill, and what she wants to kill more than you are the Silver Griffins."

"It's all just threats."

"Not if she's found an ally within their ranks." Doc Leahy sat quietly, letting that sink in.

"Do you have a name?"

"Not yet, but whoever it is, they're powerful. It's not a soldier on the ground. It's someone higher than that. The magicals' dark web is lit up with chatter about it. Rumors are everywhere."

"If the dark web knows about it, then the Silver Griffins know about it. They can do a better job of handling it."

Doc drummed his fingers impatiently on the desk. "Do you know what happens if the Silver Griffins cease to exist, especially now? Hundreds of thousands of eyes and ears that are all connected go away. That's why they pose such a threat to Ariana's plans. They can counter any kind of bullshit she comes up with to convince the human population that she has their best interests at heart. She needs undivided attention with no real counter arguments. It's kind of brilliant, really."

"You admire her, don't you?"

Doc bit the inside of his cheek. "I've known her since she was a small child. Brilliant mind, but when a magical like that grows up in a garden of poisonous weeds, don't expect a rose without some very deadly thorns. I think Ariana has been biding her time since she was a teenager. She's been observing everything, learning as much as she can and noticing what has worked and what has failed. Learning where the soft spots are and how to create even more of them."

"You make her sound very dangerous."

Doc's grey eyebrows shot up. "Oh, she is that dangerous. She doesn't have the ego of Sirius that made him brash or the lust to prove self-worth like this Wolfstan Humphrey. Yes, I've heard of him too. Ariana is patient and willing to share, and ask for help, and will take help from anyone. Like I said, even if she's planning to cut off their head later in the week."

"So, why am I here, exactly?"

Doc opened his laptop and typed in a web address, muttering a spell. A cold wind blew from his mouth, sliding into the computer and opening the site. "To get to know your real threat better. I've been watching you since you first popped up on the radar back in Austin. A Jasper Elf right under our noses and with the spark of humanity." He smiled, making a steeple with his fingers and propped his chin on them. "Darkness and light are always searching for each other. Both are needed in equal measures for the other to survive. Nature loves balance in all things. It worried me that Ariana was about to throw nature a curve." He let out a breath, a shudder passing through him. "But then I heard of you and realized once again, the scales were righting themselves. Good news, to a point." He waved to Leira, pulling over a stool, and pushing the papers on it to the floor. "Come look at what I've found."

Leira came and sat next to him, reading quickly as he clicked from one message board to another, reading high-lighted passages. Leira's eyes widened and her face warmed. "Someone is exposing where the Silver Griffins live in concentrations and where they travel. It would potentially expose hidden meeting places or..." The color drained from her face.

"Yes, or hidden vaults. Caches of artifacts hidden away for safe keeping. Or holding places for magicals that have been arrested but not yet transported. Or halls where they could be found in groups and more easily attacked. One of the biggest advantages the Silver Griffins have always had is their size and their dilution over so much territory. But everything comes with a pattern. Figure out the pattern, defeat your enemy."

Leira looked at the screen and sat back, waiting for Doc to finish. He began typing again, muttering a different spell and another ribbon of frost wove its way into the computer. A new message board appeared with available jobs. "I started seeing requests for small jobs to investigate a magical or two. No one seemed to notice them, and they didn't get much attention. But then I got curious and started to map the requests and look for similarities. At first, I could tell someone was doing a scattergun approach. Following different wizards or witches, hoping to trip over a Silver Griffin. But then, last month something changed. They became more precise and wanted more details and were willing to pay more money." He searched through the pile on his desk and pulled out a stapled sheaf of papers. "I believe the north east quadrant has already been mapped. If that's true, this is bad. This is very bad."

"This could be Wolfstan Humphrey. Still very, very bad," said Leira, taking the papers from Doc and flipping through the pages.

"I thought the same thing at first. He clearly has an agenda, but I've come to the conclusion it's not him." Doc went back to the earlier message boards and pointed at the screen. "Here, see this? Whoever it is, is creating a coalition of power. That's not Wolfstan's style. His structure is more corporate in style," said Doc, forming a tower with his hands. "All power goes to the top. Ariana understands the wider the base, the more stable the structure. Plus, notice that everyone who is hired is a wizard or a witch. I think she's getting to know them through the jobs at the same time. Like a try out. If it is her, she's been doing this even before she staged the coup. I don't even think she seized the moment. I think she created it."

"So much darkness spreading out like spider webs. I'm just one magical."

"True, and how that all adds up, I don't know. But information is power, and Ariana is probably counting on everyone being distracted by Wolfstan Humphrey and underestimating her. Don't do that. By the time we realize she's a threat every piece of her plan will be in place. Learn how to upset her apple cart now. Make her revise that plan."

Leira looked at her watch. "I have to get going. What's the new assignment?"

"This. I'm willing to put you on a retainer to keep putting these pieces together. Let me know what you find and together, we will look for ways to at least frustrate the dark families, if not stop them altogether. Then, maybe I can finally be free."

CHAPTER SEVEN

George took a seat in the booth of the Deli City Diner. Tucked carefully in the pocket of his cardigan was Yumfuck Tiberius Troll. The elderly wizard smiled up at the waitress, taking the oversized laminated menu from her. "Thank you," he said with a smile, coughing to cover up the trill coming from his pocket. The waitress tucked her chin, taking a longer look.

"Just need a little water," coughed George, taking a big sip as he tapped on his pocket.

"Uh huh," said the waitress, her hip out as she swiveled and made her way back to the kitchen.

George peeled back his pocket and looked down at the troll who was grinning up at him. "You're gonna get us caught!"

"Do they have the shepherd's pie? I've been thinking about it all week." The troll slurped, drool dribbling down his chin, catching in his fur.

"Today's special. Same every week," he said, tapping the menu. "This is going to be great," he said, rubbing his hands together. "An entire hearty meal in a bowl and this is the best place I've ever found to get one."

"Get two," said the troll, rubbing his paws together.

"You have the bowl?" George lifted the menu in front of his face as a couple sat in the booth next to him.

He looked down at the troll who was holding a small bowl over his head. "Got it!" squeaked the troll.

The waitress strode back over, pulling a pen from behind her ear. "Ready?"

George licked his lips and said it as fast as he could, doing his best to look confident. "Two shepherds pies and an iced tea with lemon on the side."

The waitress rested a hand on her hip. "You want one of those to go?"

"Nope," he said, looking her right in the eye. "Plan to eat both of them here." He smiled broadly to let her know he was sure.

The waitress' painted eyebrows slowly moved upwards. "You know we don't give any kind of prize for that. You don't get em for free and we don't put your name on any board."

George held the menu close to his chest, hiding his pocket on the other side. "I can hold more than you think."

The waitress looked him up and down and let out a laugh that turned into a cough halfway through. "I like you. Name's Delores. I always could appreciate a man who could pack it away."

George held up his hand nervously, showing Delores his wedding ring."

Delores let out a hoot of laughter. "I'm not asking you to do anything, calm down. I can still appreciate what's in the window, even if I'm not buying. Okay, two shepherds' pies and an iced tea, lemon on the side coming up." She turned on her heel, not waiting for an answer. "Two more shepherds, Jack!" she shouted in the direction of the kitchen. A beefy cook with a stained apron leaned out of the order window and gave a quick nod, turning his back.

George looked down at the troll. "Whew. That was close."

"She likes you."

"She appreciates your appetite."   .

The troll smiled and let out a whistle. George startled and looked up in time to see Delores give him a wink before disappearing into the kitchen.

"Why do I feel like I'm eating my last supper?" George nervously moved the silverware around, trying not to look at the couple in the next booth. They were smiling at him and nudging each other. "Kids," muttered George.

It wasn't long before Delores had come back with the order, sliding the plates off a large tray. "The plates are hot so be careful," she said, setting down the iced tea. "Give it a minute to cool off or you'll burn your tongue. Just a suggestion," she said, winking again. "Hold your horses," she yelled to a man waving his arm at a table. "I can see you. I'm not blind, you know." She walked away as George broke the top of the mashed potatoes with a spoon, letting out the steam.

"Yummmmm...," said the troll. "Gimme, gimme motherfucker!"

George tried to smile at the couple who were laughing, the young man raising his glass in a toast. A woman at a nearby table covered her ten year old son's ears with her hands. The boy rolled his eyes and kept eating his sandwich.

George looked down at his pocket, speaking out the side of his mouth. "It's still hot."

"Try me," said the troll. "I can take it. Come on, come on!" The troll's voice was growing louder, and others were starting to look at George.

George got a small amount loaded on the spoon. "Portia said this was a bad idea, but noooooo. I said how hard can it be to sneak a five inch fur ball into a diner. He'll love it, I said." He opened his pocket and the troll held up his bowl as George dropped it in. Yumfuck tilted the bowl back and swallowed and held the bowl up again.

"Oh geez," said George. "This is gonna take forever."

"Just slide her on in. I can take it." Yumfuck put down the bowl and opened his mouth wide. He looked up at George and nodded. "Let's do this," he said, opening just a skosh wider.

George stared at the wide open mouth and the tiny pointed teeth. He looked back at the kitchen and back at the troll who was frantically waving his paws.

"Why not?" he asked, holding a napkin around the edge of the plate and scooting it toward the edge. "Bottoms up!" He poured some of the hot mixture of beef and peas and mashed potatoes into the troll's mouth, marveling at how quickly it disappeared. "More?" George snorted with laughter and tilted the plate again, letting the mixture spill out till the plate was empty.

"Do you need a refill?"

George looked up, surprised, at Delores standing at the table with a pitcher of iced tea. He carefully pushed the empty plate away from the edge and said, "Not just yet. I've been busy."

"I can see that. Your tongue must be numb from those hot potatoes."

A loud belch emanated from George's pocket and he covered his mouth, muttering, "Excuse me."

"No need. It's nice to see someone really appreciate the cooking. I'll tell Jack. You gonna need dessert? I mean, I would have sworn you wouldn't have any room, skinny thing like you, but sometimes it's the tall and lean ones that fool you." Delores wandered off, still muttering to herself.

George broke the top of the mashed potatoes on the second plate trying not to make eye contact with anyone. He felt Yumfuck stirring in his pocket and looked down, peeking in his pocket to find the troll curled up in a ball, fast asleep. "Huh, maybe I was right after all. Not so hard," said George, sliding a spoonful in his mouth. "Hot, hot, hot..." He poured cold water in his mouth and waved his hand over the plate. "Maybe wait a little longer."

Yumfuck grew to three feet tall and settled in at his desk, his belly still full of warm mashed potatoes and peas. He pulled out a paper and pen and tapped the pen against his sharp, pointy teeth before starting to write.

Dear Hagan,

    It was a big day. I got to try shepherd's pie. Best thing ever, maybe even better than Cheetos. Have you tried it?

. . .

The troll drew two boxes with *yes* next to one, and *no* next to the other.

How are you doing at the sanctuary? I hope to visit soon. I've made a new friend. A troll friend! Don't worry, you're still my bestie for life. Jackson got himself a troll and he promised he'd come and visit with him. Still no name for him yet, but something will come up. The project I told you about is coming along. Thanks for keeping my secret. Leira is hot on my trail but so far, she has no idea. Correk is fine. He's gotten a little better at hiding his snacks, but that just adds to the excitement. I'll find the stash soon enough.

Yumfuck sighed and sat back in the chair. Nothing else was coming to him and he set the pen down. "I'll finish later. Maybe something exciting will happen. Who knows?"

CHAPTER EIGHT

The cement foundation and framework of the new club house was already in place. Lucius stood out in front of it, admiring the building, dressed in jeans and a t-shirt that was almost too small. "Nice duds there, Lucius." A young female shifter walked by him, giving him a wink.

Lucius reddened, crossing his arms over his chest and trying to make a scowl, but it kept turning into a smile.

"Nice to know even an eight hundred year old Light Elf can adapt." Turner Underwood appeared just behind him, tapping his cane.

"Has anyone ever told you that's an annoying habit. Need to put a bell on you somewhere." Lucius stood up straighter, the t-shirt pulling across his chest.

Turner smiled, patting his old friend on the back. "It's okay to just be happy, Lucius. Hang around long enough with these young shifters from the suburbs and it'll rub off on you. You'll even get used to it. He nodded toward a group of them standing in the middle of the skeleton of the building. "They're really learning how to work together. You're doing a great job as an alpha, Lucius."

Lucius grunted but the smile returned, if only to a corner of his mouth. He turned to say something to Turner, but the old Fixer was already gone. "Damn it, Turner!" Lucius growled but looked up at the new construction and let out a contented sigh, surprising himself.

"Looks pretty good doesn't it?" A male shifter walked by him in green golf pants and a pink Izod shirt, hurrying over to the group. Lucius looked confused, watching the shifter and then looking down at his t-shirt.

"I'm here and I brought donuts!" The new arrival held up a large bag as a cheer went up from the group.

"Derby's here!"

Derby handed over the bag and made his way inside the cluster. The shifters were gathered around one middle-aged shifter who was holding his phone out so they could all see the screen.

"What does this button do, Felix?" A shifter with long, bony fingers reached out but Felix slapped his hand.

"We talked about this Joey. Ask questions first. It's just the beta." He looked sideways at Joey, muttering, "A shifter with impulse control issues. What next?"

"Aw, put your fur down, Felix." Joey smiled, waiting for a response, but Felix just rolled his eyes.

Another shifter pointed at the screen. "Hey, you're getting a text from your wife. Make sure you get the good kind of toilet paper."

The small group started laughing and jostling Felix who

finally gave in and smiled. "You are all just jealous of a happy marriage."

"Look, we already have over a hundred users," said Derby, clapping his hands together.

"Yeah, from all over the state. It's actually working," said Joey. "Okay, okay, relax. I'm not touching anything on your phone. Look, I have the same app on mine." He held up his phone and scrolled through the posts. "Hey, there's a post here about a run through Shenandoah National Forest this weekend after it closes. That could be fun."

Felix rolled his eyes but stopped mid-way when he saw Derby's face. His face was glistening with sweat and he looked like he was fighting back pain. "Derby, you okay? Something wrong? Everybody back up and give him room." Felix put up an arm, pushing people into a wider circle as Derby started to grunt. He bent over at the waist, his hands on his knees. Thick, wiry hairs began to sprout on the back of his hands. "Fuck!" he said, through gritted teeth. "What's happening? I can't control it?"

"He's been poisoned!"

"It's happened again."

"How did someone get to him here?"

"Joey, he just got here. Somebody must have gotten to him at the donut place."

"Isn't that like sacrilegious? I mean... donuts."

Two shifters holding donuts immediately dropped them on the ground.

Lucius came barreling through the middle of the crowd and stood over Derby, not sure what to do.

A sudden wind came up, blowing dust in everyone's

face. Lucius tried to shield his eyes, placing himself between the wind and his pack.

When the air was still again, Correk was there, kneeling over Derby who had collapsed to the cement floor.

"What is with you Fixers? You can't just appear like a normal magical?"

Correk ignored Lucius and pulled out the bowl he had borrowed from his father. Derby was already shifting, tearing his nice golf pants, jerking in pain. Correk took the bowl in one hand and placed his other hand over Derby, repeating the spell he used before. The bowl quivered in Correk's hand as Derby let out an anguished cry and fell back.

It was over before it had really started. He was breathing hard, quickly transforming back into human form. Correk stood, holding the bowl out for Lucius. "Take good care of the relic. It's a temporary fix that should help if there's a sudden need."

Joey helped Derby sit up and poked Correk in the arm. "Won't you just show up?"

"Joey, don't poke a Fixer," said Felix. The others looked at each other nervously.

Correk waited till Joey was standing and he could look him calmly in the eye. "This is just the beginning of the troubles, Joey. Things are getting more complicated and there may be more than one fire or even ten fires to put out at the same time. We are all going to have to work together." His voice was steady and even as he put a heavy hand on Joey's shoulder. "You're going to need to be there for each other."

Joey held up his phone, his hand shaking a little. "We have an app for that."

"That's a good start, Joey."

"Hey, Lucius, can I get that bowl?" A shifter wearing thick glasses and thinning hair stepped forward. "I work in a lab and I can test all of this evidence. If I find something the bowl may help figure out how it works." The man went to pick up the donuts but Correk stopped him. He pulled out a grey silicone bag from his satchel and handed it to him. "Use this," said Correk. "Keep the samples in this bag till you have on protective gear."

Lucius pulled Correk aside, the scowl back on his face. "We have to do more than this." He shook his head. "I'm not going to just respond to whatever happens. I want to rout whoever is causing it in the first place. I want Wolfstan Humphrey."

"Then we follow the clues we have till we can prove it's him. It's a different world, Lucius. We don't hunt down who we think may be responsible. We actually figure that out first."

"I liked my way better," growled the Alpha.

"Look at your pack, Lucius. You start a war with Wolfstan, most of them won't make it. That's not a great leader. It's not even a good one. Start thinking big picture and you'll be more useful to them. Lean on their abilities and what they can contribute. It will make your entire pack formidable and a very good ally."

"You've grown in this past year, Correk. It's that Berens woman, isn't it?"

Correk pulled a ball of light apart, opening a portal.

"Always and forever," he said, as he stepped through to the hallway of his house. "Delegate Lucius and admit when you don't know something. Wolfstan is too strong for us to remain stubborn." He let the portal shut behind him without waiting for a reply.

CHAPTER NINE

"I'll only be gone for a half hour. Not even the full stretch." Lois held out the black patent leather purse as Mabel stared at her, nervously biting her lip. "Put out your hand, Mabel. This hand off isn't going to work unless you do."

Patsy stood between them, looking back and forth and occasionally opening her mouth to say something. But Lois raised a finger in the air and that was all it took for Patsy to hesitate. Still, she would screw up her face and try again, letting out short gasps and clearing her throat.

Mabel swallowed hard and reluctantly stretched out her right arm as Lois carefully slid the handles in place and left the purse dangling. Mabel was still biting her lip but looked somewhat surprised and relieved. "Not as heavy as I thought it would be."

Lois drew her brows together, a little annoyed. "I don't know whether to be impressed that you think I have some kind of super magical strength or dismayed that you didn't just ask."

Mabel started opening and shutting her mouth to say something, inadvertently making herself a mirror image of Patsy.

"For Pete's sake, both of you! If you're going to be in the Silver Griffins, you're going to have to buck up a hell of a lot more." Lois rolled her eyes and patted Mabel hard on the back. "Spit it out. What is it?"

Mabel licked her lips and started slowly. "It's just that..." She held up her arm, the purse gently swaying, making Mabel's eyes grow wider. She held the purse closer and kept going. "This is kind of the whole kit and kaboodle for the Silver Griffins. It's a lot of responsibility."

"I'm glad you can see that," said Lois, keeping her voice more even. "But it's also only for thirty minutes. You do recognize I'm not the entire organization, right?"

Mabel eagerly nodded her head.

"Well, then we're going to have to be able to lean on each other."

"What if someone asks her why she's got your purse?" Patsy spit out the words till they all ran together.

"You two are worrying too much. It's thirty freakin minutes. Fine." Lois threw up her hands. "If anyone asks, tell them..." Lois let out a sigh, tapping a finger against her cheek. "Tell them..."

"See? Not so easy. And what happened to not using the zoetrope outside of the vault" said Patsy, pulling out her wand just in case Lois had an idea to spark her for even bringing it up.

"Tell them I'm in the ladies' room taking care of old age lady parts." Lois gave a satisfied nod.

Mabel turned pale and looked at the purse, her eyes

wide. Patsy came close to spitting out the caramel she was nursing in her cheek and snorted with laughter. "That's aggressive, but I have to admit, effective. I'd like to see the balls on the one who comes up with a follow up inquiry."

"Then we're all agreed." Lois lifted the zoetrope off her desk along with a strip of paper with a sequence of poses of a pale grey and blue swallow printed on it. Lois gently patted Mabel's arm. "I'll be back before you know it." She looked at how tightly Mabel was holding the purse. "You can hold it a little looser, dear. The contents don't actually sway back and forth. The magic keeps everything stable. Okay, I'm off." She spun the zoetrope as fast as she could before anyone could say anything else and was transformed into a swallow, already flapping her wings.

"This thing would make a good Christmas present," muttered Patsy. "To me."

The small bird darted out of Lois' office and kept to the top of the hallway, heading for the large cafeteria. It was tucked on the third floor away from tourists who might wander in for a play. The bird came to rest on the thin metal rods that held up the large industrial lights in the high ceiling. She was just above the tables, crowded with wizards and witches busy eating and sharing gossip.

"Oh, a bird!" A witch took out her wand and flicked it, opening a tall window on the far side of the room. She swirled it around, above her head and sent a small cyclone to pick up the swallow and send it toward the window. But the bird was faster and ducked out of the way, soaring to another light and hiding behind the round silver fixture.

"Missed again, Ellen. Close the window, will you? This is Chicago." The heavyset witch turned back to her neighbor as Ellen grimaced, but shut the window, giving up on the swallow. "Now finish your story, Erickson. Where have you been lately? I mean, I know you can't tell us mission stuff, but you've been pretty MIA, even for you." The witch leaned her head on her hand, her elbow on the table.

Erickson took another bite of his sandwich, looking around the room, chewing slowly.

"Leave him alone Bartley. He clearly doesn't want to say. Hey, I heard that the new boss is redoing her office in early candy store. Man, that is using your noodle. To hell with some big new sofa. Bring on the glass jars of sour patch kids."

"You think they'll ever do anything about the old vault?" A skinny wizard with blonde highlights picked at his potato chips. "That thing is a disaster waiting to happen."

"Hey, can I have your chips?" asked Ellen.

"It's been reinforced," said Bartley, shifting in her seat. "It'll be fine. It's worked this long and if the dark families could have taken it out by now, they would have. Erickson, what do you think? Are you even paying attention?"

Erickson was checking his phone again, scrolling through the listings on the database, waiting for one of his alerts to pay off. "What?" he asked, jerking his head up, but not really looking at anyone. "Uh, I have no idea."

Bartley narrowed her gaze, giving him a longer look, sliding her chips over to Ellen. "Bottom line, we will survive. Silver Griffins stick together. It's the secret sauce to our survival."

CHAPTER TEN

Ariana stood in the back of the meeting room. Young witches and wizards were sitting around the table, their heads bent toward computer screens. A satisfied warmth spread through her chest. "This is working," she whispered.

Agnes came to the large doorway and stood in the center watching, her arms crossed. "Your job is to successfully manage the families," she finally said.

"Agnes, that limited thinking is exactly why you're no longer in charge. The world is connected in new and powerful ways that go far beyond magic. Hell, technology is a kind of magic and if we're not a part of it, we're going to get run over by it."

"Since when did good leadership equate with common popularity?" Agnes wrinkled her nose like there was a stench in the air.

Ariana slowly walked toward Agnes as a few of the witches along one side of the long table glanced up, and quickly looked away again. The young head of the families unfurled one hand, one finger at a time, the sharp red nails catching the sunlight from the tall windows. She let out a long breath, flicking her long hair behind her shoulder, in no hurry to cross the room. At the last moment, she picked up her wand, a rare elm variety and held it lightly, holding Agnes' gaze.

"Agnes, was your plan to just ignore the rest of the world? To isolate us from everything and everyone and just wait for the gates to close again? That would have only taken, what, another twenty thousand years?" She came within a few feet of the older witch. "I can't decide if it was fear or ignorance that kept you so small. Either way, your time has passed and at the moment you are more a hindrance than an asset."

"Pay heed, Ariana. Our misfortunes have always come more from the magical side of things than humans. If you insist on taking your focus off what other magicals are doing... Leira Berens. Wolfstan Humphrey. The Silver Griffins. That's just the organized list and doesn't include the crazier side of our world." Ariana started to cut her off, but Agnes raised her hand sharply. "If you insist on ignoring thousands of years of experience to chart this new course, you will stand alone on top of the wreckage of what we once were and you alone will take the full brunt of the responsibility." Agnes turned, not waiting for a response.

A murmur arose behind Ariana making her clench her wand tightly. She snapped it in the air, slamming the doors and bringing the noise to a stop. "When will that damn woman realize we are no longer in the dark ages?" Ariana screamed, shaking her hands over her head. She curled her hands into fists at her side, her long nails pressing into her palms. "Steady, steady," she muttered, willing herself to calm down, pressing her lips together. "Keep the vision." She closed her eyes, smoothing her hair on her shoulders and opened them, putting the same steady smile on her face that never reached her eyes.

She spun around, dancing the wand through the air making the wizards closest to her flinch even as they tried to hide it.

"Tell me, how are we doing with our fundraiser?"

A young wizard with blonde hair cleared his throat. "We've raised thirty thousand so far to make sure every human has internet access. No more dead spots when we're done."

"And the gala?"

A witch with a brown ponytail on the top of her head that formed a fountain of hair, stood up abruptly, chattering away. "The invitations were hand delivered to the guest list a week ago, except for the few you asked to have delivered at the last minute. Those are being dropped off as we speak to our frenemies. The caterer is nailed down, and we are awaiting word on the venue."

Ariana arched a brow, pursing her lips. The witch sputtered and nodded several times. "Of course, I'll follow up with the place and offer more if that's what it takes." She sat down just as precipitously and started typing.

A dark haired wizard leaned back from his computer, brushing long bangs out of his face and smiling devilishly at Ariana. "I suppose posting is next." He sat up in his chair. "We've got a few hashtags trending. Instagathering.

ConnectionKarma. VelvetRopeAccess. That last one is my favorite."

"Harry, I'm glad you've found a way to entertain yourself that doesn't involve blowing things up, dear little brother. But how about you tell me what you know I want to hear?" Ariana tapped him on the shoulder with her wand sending an electrical current through him, grounding in the floor.

Harry winced, the smile turning into a grimace. "Always a stickler. That's why there's dust gathering between your..."

Ariana shocked him again. "Stick to the topic, or else, and this time you won't have mummy to save you."

Harry rolled his shoulder and glowered at the witch next to him who was barely suppressing a smile. "Fine. We're up to a million likes overall and the posts are being shared thousands of times. The general feeling is that it's about time someone try to connect everyone and just hand out internet access to the poor or rural areas." Harry's smile was starting to return. "It's really kind of genius. They'll never realize there's just a little bit of dark magic sailing into their lives every time they log on."

"Facts are really more subjective than most people care to admit. Win their minds, fuck their hearts," said Ariana, walking past her brother. "Uncle Felix have you made the donation yet?"

An older lean wizard in a bespoke suit stepped out of the shadows. His dark hair was slicked back exposing a sharp widow's peak on his forehead. "The local DC animal shelters have received a very generous donation in your name with a request that it be used to help as many dogs as possible. We made sure to let Lucius know. Clever, niece, to be making friends with shifters. That alliance may someday prove to be very effective. They blend in so well with the humans." He snorted with a short laugh. "Hell, half of them used to be human. You'd think they'd blame all of us for what happened to them, but clever, clever girl."

Ariana patiently watched her favorite relative walk around the table, still talking. He was the only magical anyone knew of that she tolerated so well.

"You managed to convince them it was all Sirius and Juliana's idea." He shook his head, laughing again. "You would have made a good carny."

"It was all their backward idea. They have no imagination."

Uncle Felix did a small pirouette, pointing a lean, bony finger in the air. "Or a gypsy like your cousin, Marnie," he said, ignoring what she said, as usual. 'Good people, gypsies. They practice very old dark magic with the herbs and weeds. Too bad they don't like to share knowledge. Ah well, something to think about on another day."

"Were you able to find enough items for the silent auction?" Ariana smiled, dimples appearing in her cheeks. A witch smiled up at her, relaxing at her spot until Ariana returned the gesture with a growl.

Uncle Felix leaned back his head and laughed, patting the nearest wizard hard on the back. "Classic Ariana! Yes, of course I found enough items. We've been collecting artifacts for thousands of years. It's about time we had an upscale yard sale. Oooh, there's another hashtag for you Harry," he said, smiling and pointing at his nephew. "UpscaleYardSale. Do it!"

Ariana snapped her fingers sharply, sending an energy pulse through the room, creating wavy lines that reverberated around everything. A witch covered her mouth, turning her head and swallowing hard to stop from throwing up her lunch. Uncle Felix shut his eyes for a moment and braced himself to stop from falling over.

"Now that I have your full attention." Ariana looked at her uncle, finally tired of his side show. "Did you get the grand prize?"

Uncle Felix opened his eyes again and coughed briefly, patting his lips with his fist. "Of course, I did. Have I ever failed you, unlike young Harry here?" He walked back into the shadows briefly and reemerged holding a shallow pewter plate. "Looks so plain, doesn't it? Infernal piece of dinnerware." He walked to a corner of the table and picked up a half-filled open water bottle, splashing the bottom of the plate. "Gaze into the water and you can see your fate, if you stay on the course you've set. Change one thing, watch the events unfold differently."

Harry got up, licking his lips, walking closer to Uncle Felix with his hands on his hips. "Why would you call that infernal? Sounds very, very useful."

Ariana rolled her eyes, already smiling again at her uncle. "Every magical known to have used the plate has gotten hypnotized by knowing the outcome. They become frozen in place, refusing to do anything. It's a trap. A damnable trap," she said with delight.

Uncle Felix tilted the plate to one side, letting the water drain out. A witch caught her reflection and gasped. She saw herself lying still on a battlefield, a broken wand at her side. The petite blonde stared back at the computer screen, her eyes filling as Ariana tapped her shoulder. "Mindy here gets it. Don't worry, it's just a prediction of what could happen. Change one thing and the outcome disappears."

Mindy bit her trembling lower lip and slowly got up, went to the large door and pulled it open, leaving the great hall.

"Already changing things, Mindy. Well done."

"I can't say as I blame her, but you're probably going to need a replacement, Ariana, for that seat." Uncle Felix smiled, holding the plate closer to his chest. "This prize should bring a pretty penny at the gala. I wonder who will win it."

"The perfect item. It will curse whoever gets it, but it will be much later before they realize it. The human world will benefit from the proceeds and thank us. Even the Silver Griffins will find it hard to say anything."

"Oh, but they'll try my favorite niece. They will try."

CHAPTER ELEVEN

Winland Underwood was a chip off her father's block. She wasn't about to sit around in a city from a hundred years ago and wait for someone else to solve her problems. No sir, she was going to figure out how to get the ball rolling.

That's what had brought her to the door of the mansion, looking out at the busy DC street. She hovered and teetered, wondering for just a second if this was a good idea. "It's an idea," she said firmly, nodding her head. A hastily thought out idea without a lot of planning, but an idea. It would have to do.

She had sat in her father's townhouse long enough, listening to him rail about a magical chasing down other magicals. She knew there was just a little bit of a father's indignation mixed in with an old Fixer's instinct to protect. But in the end, no plan had taken shape and all Winland had gotten were promises that living inside of a city that was inside of a building wouldn't go on forever. But for a magical, even that promise could still add up to a very long time.

There had to be something more that could be done.

In his fury, Turner had rumbled to himself when he thought he was alone about a Silver Griffin being at the heart of things. It gave Winland an idea.

"I've waited long enough to be free and find my own way," she muttered, starting down the steps.

Winland Underwood had learned a few tricks from her father over the years, mostly at his insistence. One of them was how to follow him without getting caught. She'd been doing it since she was nine years old and successfully since she was thirteen.

In her hand was one of his canes, a necessary accessory for this particular trick. A hard hickory cane with a resting silver eagle for a handle.

"Time to go." Before she could think about it again, she tapped the cane hard on the ground and whispered the short spell, with a slight adjustment.

She magically sent herself where Turner Underwood had been, instead of where he was now. It took her to the small town of Belle Haven, Virginia in front of the Idle Hour Theatre. "What or who was here before?" she asked, looking up at the tall, narrow sign.

A local farmer in dusty overalls walked by her, looking her up and down. She was wearing the high waisted navy skirt and puffy blouse, with her hair pinned loosely on top and buttoned up boots. More appropriate for another century. "Takes all kinds, I guess," he said, making his way toward the center of town.

Winland ignored him and made a point of searching for

her father's brilliant trail of silver and gold sparkles. Invisible to most magicals but not Winland and not with his cane in her hand.

She easily found it and followed his footsteps, winding around the nearby blocks, disappearing in spots and reappearing. "There it is," she said triumphantly when she came across the missing ingredient to make her plan work.

A green trail of fading magic with flecks of black growing in it. A Silver Griffin's magic that was becoming tainted. Winland knelt and ran her hand across the stream. Just as she suspected, the tracers had been stripped out of it. It was a traitor who knew how to cover their tracks, even from a Fixer. A seasoned Silver Griffin operative.

"Well then, I guess we have to tempt you to come to me."

Winland was breathing harder, her chest rising and falling as she swirled the cane in her father's magic and mixed it with the remnants of the traitor, creating a whirlpool. "Ollie, ollie, oxen free." An old spell used to find children and would work just as well here to attract the miscreant.

The wind picked up, blowing back the wisps of hair hanging down around her face. Anyone else looking out their window would have seen a woman in costume standing in the middle of a strange windstorm that was confined to that spot right there. But Winland could see the magic blending together around her. The boost from her father's energy helped it sail out to its intended target, disappearing over the horizon. It wouldn't be long now before it arrived at his doorstep, whoever he was.

The swallow flew lower where it was easier to hear in the large cafeteria, dodging flailing arms and wands.

"There goes your bird, Ellen!" called out a witch at a nearby table, her hands over her food.

Erickson abruptly stood, growing flush.

"Hey Erickson, where are you going?" Bartley drank the rest of her soda, starting to get up to follow him. "Is there a new mission?"

"I... uh... I have to take this." He was quickly scrolling past the alert to hide the blinking red banner from the others. A target at last. He got up quickly and walked across the large cafeteria.

"That was abrupt," said the skinny wizard.

"That's life at the top of the SG's!" shouted Bartley, a fist in the air, still watching Erickson leave.

The swallow circled the ceiling and ducked out of the hall, looking for Erickson. The bird caught up with him at the end of a long hall dotted on either side by offices with their doors mostly closed. He was already stepping through a hastily made portal, pulling at the sides and letting it snap shut behind him in a flurry of sparks. He was making sure no one followed him. The bird tweeted in frustration but flew back, swooping up the stairs toward her office, full of questions.

Erickson turned around in a circle, standing in the center of the street in Belle Haven. He gave a nod to the same farmer who was retracing his steps along a familiar path he'd been taking for years.

"Is there some kind of cosplay in town today?" The farmer scratched his head but kept walking, carrying a grocery bag balanced in his other arm.

"It's just a suit," said Erickson with a tinge of annoyance. "A really nice suit."

"Like I said." The older farmer shifted the bag and shook his head, turning his back. He quietly pulled an old weathered oak wand out of a front pocket and held it close to the bag. On the inside of his wrinkled wrist was a tattoo of two faded S's intertwined. He kept walking, keeping a steady pace, but there was a steady hum of energy across the back of his neck. Something wasn't right.

Erickson was too distracted to notice.

The balding farmer made it to the small side street and kept walking. The road curved slightly to the right, hiding him from view. He finally stopped when he got to the far side of the first small house. He put down his groceries out of sight of the square and crept back, hugging the side of the house. He started to crouch and felt his knees protest, choosing instead to stay upright. "Oh, here we go." An old recognizable rush of adrenaline poured through him. He made small circles with his wand, creating a ward to keep others from wanting to venture closer to the square.

Winland Underwood stepped out from the side of the theater into the sunlight, her eyes already glowing and a fireball in her hand. "Are you looking for me?"

Erickson spun around, surprised. His anger was getting the better of him. So many years waiting for revenge had taken its toll. He was taken aback by Winland's outfit but quickly let it go. There were more important things to focus on, at last. "Your kind," he said, through gritted teeth. "You don't deserve protection." He raised his wand to strike but Winland gave a hard tap to the cane and disappeared, reappearing behind him.

"Who appointed you our judge and jury?" she shouted. Erickson turned again, confused. The farmer watched, his mouth hanging open, but his wand still at the ready.

Erickson didn't wait this time and swung his wand around, releasing a ropey light of fire slicing across the square.

Winland lifted the cane in front of her body, holding it vertically. She swung it in a circle at the last moment, catching the fire around the stem. The heat made her wince in pain, but she kept her grip. The fire built into a large ball that slipped off the cane at the bottom. It gave one hard bounce on the road before Winland swung the cane, striking it hard.

The fireball raced across the divide like an earthbound meteor, barely missing Erickson but leaving him with a burn mark down the sleeve of his jacket. The wizard looked shaken, hesitating for a second before using his wand again to send a pulse of energy.

But it was long enough for the retired Silver Griffin in the shadows to finally use his wand. He whispered, "Ad missori dandum salvis."

The wave bent and curled, doing its best to obey two practitioners of magic. The air crackled as the wave compressed, undulating in a narrowing column, shaking the ground. Winland looked confused but used the opportunity to sail a fireball around the column, striking

Erickson this time squarely in the chest. He landed on his back, the wind knocked out of him, barely holding on to his wand.

The wave snapped, released from one side unexpectedly and tore at the ground beneath it, creating a sudden chasm. Erickson rolled onto his knees, wounded and unable to fight. He opened a portal as quickly as he could, pulling at the sides.

Another portal was opening closer to Winland. She wasn't sure where to put her attention and braced herself to fight in two directions.

Correk stepped through, assessing the battlefield and put himself between Winland and the wave of energy that was still out of control. Erickson pitched himself forward into the portal opening he had created and pulled at the sides. But not before locking eyes with Correk whose eyes widened. "You?" asked Correk, his brow furrowing.

Erickson hung his head as the portal closed and sparks danced on the ground, close to the chasm.

The farmer lowered his wand, releasing his side of the spell as the wave slowly rolled down to a vibration and then disappeared altogether. The old wizard then went back to pick up his groceries and go on his way. He could call his old friend, Lois when he got home. "It's been too long since I've talked to her anyway."

Correk moved his hands in a counterclockwise motion, his eyes glowing as the earth pulled itself back together, erasing the deep crack.

Winland Underwood waited till the ground was still to say anything. "I had to do it. I needed to be free," she said, gripping the cane.

"I understand and I think you actually did us a favor. It might have taken us longer to figure out at least one traitor in our midst. However, your father may see things differently."

"He probably will and it's still okay. This was my decision to make. I'll stand by it," she said, tapping the cane hard on the ground. She was gone without another word, leaving Correk standing there by himself.

"What just happened?" He shook his head. "Things are getting out of control," he muttered as he opened a portal back to his own hallway. The portal widened and he saw Leira smiling and holding a beer. "You'll never believe what I just saw," he said, stepping through and taking the beer. "I know who's the traitor in the Silver Griffins."

"Wow, I'm all ears," said Leira as the portal closed.

CHAPTER TWELVE

Wolfstan sat at the lower table, looking up at the bank of Senators gazing at him from the perch behind the imposing wooden dais. He was doing his best to let go of his recent losses and focus on the prize at hand. *Let the magical world rot. Oriceran and the dark families. This is more important.*

His fingers were laced together under the table to steady his nerves. He wasn't used to being this tentative, but this time he could feel something new and different headed his way. A victory, at last.

"Mr. Humphrey," said Senator Thatcher, glancing to his right and then his left. "After much discussion, we have decided to..." He paused, clearing his throat, a somber look on his face. "To temporarily give you a seat on this committee."

It was all Wolfstan could do to stay in his seat. He gripped his fingers tighter and pressed his lips together to stop himself from shouting with joy.

"I'm going to emphasize for you, Mr. Wolfstan that this

is temporary and can end at any moment of our choosing. But for today, and not for public consumption, we are offering you an advisory role. You will not have voting privileges and we may ignore your advice. Do you understand?"

Wolfstan felt a little of the joy slip away. No voting rights.

The Senators shifted in their seats, Senator Bleeden tapping his pen against the wooden top of the dais. Senator Thatcher took a sip of water, appearing in no hurry for an answer. Wolfstan finally gave a nod and felt the thrill return, zipping around in his chest. A door had not only finally opened for him, he was being given a seat.

"Thank you everyone. I humbly accept and I'm at your disposal. Where do we start?"

"When do we get to fly again?" Patsy was staring at the jars of candy in Lois' office, trying to decide. Sweet or sour.

"I told you, we can't use the zoetrope willy nilly." Lois sat back in her chair, lost in thought, pushing her glasses back up her nose.

Patsy finally settled on a small box of Junior Mints, prying open one end and pouring the contents into her mouth, mashing them down. "One time," she slurped through chocolate and mint creme. She poked Lois' arm leaving a small dot of dark chocolate. Her face registered surprise but she hid it quickly, swallowing the rest of the candy and wiping her hands on a nearby napkin. "Just one more."

"You know I'm gonna give in eventually, but not today. I have bigger things on my mind." Lois pulled out the invitation on heavy gold card stock with black lettering.

"Ooooh, what's this? Looks like a fancy party. And we're invited!" chirped Patsy.

"Look closer at who's hosting the gala."

Patsy squinted and looked at the small print near the bottom. "Oh. My. Well, that is something. The dark families are throwing a fancy shindig and they've invited the Silver Griffins. Ooh, I see they waited till the last moment to invite us. The gala is tonight." She held up the invitation. "This could be good news or a weird call to arms. Hard to know with these younger magicals."

"It gets better. There was an insert," said Lois, holding up a smaller card. "There's a silent auction of artifacts to benefit some new charity that Ariana has started. Dark family artifacts. Imagine what they're going to pull out and release into the world."

"This is getting more interesting by the moment. We're going, of course."

"Most definitely. I wouldn't miss this new chapter for just about anything. I can't remember the last time this many magicals gathered in one place. That's part of what worries me."

"We'll go packing our fanciest wands and treat the whole ballroom like a potential battlefield. Nothing new for us."

Lois broke into a grin and stood up. "This is why you're my best friend. Hey, what's this?" she asked, noticing the chocolate stain on her sleeve. "Were you even gonna tell me?"

"Not unless I had to," said Patsy, ducking as a tiny spray of fireballs flew over her head. "Earl will get it out. He always does," said Patsy, returning fire.

Lois moved the purse out of the way just in time, a pea-sized fireball bouncing harmlessly off the zoetrope, sparking as it rolled across her desk. She was laughing so hard she got a stitch in her side. "How do you manage to do that, Patsy. I should be down in the dumps with all these problems."

Patsy shrugged and held up her wand, just in case. "That's my job, Lois. That's always been my job. Now, what are you gonna wear to this thing. I'm thinking of a fuchsia number I have that really shows off my good side."

"How does a dress show off just one side? Never mind. Sounds perfect," said Lois, smiling, still holding the invitation. An alarm went off on the sideboard behind Lois, flashing a red light and emitting a high pitched whine. Lois dropped the invitation and slammed her hand down on the button to stop the noise.

"What the hell is that?" asked Patsy, her hands over her ears.

"It's not good, that's for sure. A Silver Griffins agent has been captured. Third one this week. Someone has outed us to our enemies."

"Any patterns?"

"Only a broad one. They were all on the East Coast but no cluster. That can't be. No one would betray us like that, surely. Come on Patsy, we need to work a little faster."

Lois' phone rang and she picked it up. "Fenmore, it's been a month of Sundays since I've heard from you. What gives in Belle Haven?" The color drained from Lois' face.

"You are still a very useful ally to the Silver Griffins, Fenmore. Thank you. I'll be in touch. Say hello to Alice for me."

"What was that?" Patsy stood still, a green M&M halfway to her mouth. "You don't look so good."

"You ever have something confirmed that you hoped like hell would turn out to be wrong? I have a good idea about who is the turncoat in our operation."

"Who's the fink? Name him!" Patsy squeezed the M&M till it was crushed, surprising herself.

"Erickson. I trusted him. Lacey trusted him. What has he done? What harm has he caused?"

CHAPTER THIRTEEN

Leira came out of the bathroom, fixing the back of the large hoop earring. She was wearing a long, deep red dress with a halter top that showed off her shoulders and clung to her curves. Correk stopped braiding his blonde hair and stared, his mouth hanging open.

"What is it? Did I spill something?" Leira turned around in a circle, showing off the large bow at the back of her neck, the ends trailing down to the floor.

"You... You are more beautiful every day," Correk choked out.

Leira stopped twirling and smiled, letting out a relieved sigh. "I'm so glad every day that the king of Oriceran ordered you to follow me everywhere."

Correk stepped closer, wrapping his arms around her, letting them slide lower. "We could be late."

"And miss whatever trap Ariana is setting for us? No way." She smiled, tilting her chin up to kiss him, sliding her tongue between his teeth. "Don't wrinkle the dress," she said, turning her head to look back. I don't want to walk in with two hand imprints on my ass."

"There are worse things," said Correk, not letting go.

"Okay, a little late. Help me out of this thing. Carefully."

Correk whispered something under his breath and snapped his fingers, the dress disappearing from her body and reappearing on the hangar hooked on the closet door. "Turner Underwood taught me that one."

"Of course, he did. That's got to be one of his top five spells. Now, where were we?" she asked, as he picked her up and gently laid her on the bed. "Never use that one on anyone else," she said as he climbed onto the bed.

"Only you. For a hundred more years, and then a hundred more, only you."

Correk straightened his tie and bent his arm for Leira to slide her hand inside as they walked into the restored Howard Theater on T Street. The lobby was already filling with people in long gowns and tuxedos greeting each other and laughing. Leira and Correk smiled at each other as they moved toward a long table. A young witch was checking in guests as they waited behind a Wood Elf who was giving his name. "Laxon. The name is Laxon," he said curtly, as the witch ran a finger up and down the list. "Try under L," he said. The witch finally found it and gave a nod, the signal to the guards to let the Elf pass.

Leira started to say her name. "Leira..."

"No need to check in these two!" Ariana's voice carried easily over the hum of the crowd. "Leira, Correk, I'm so glad you could make it and on such short notice." Ariana was in a bright yellow dress with billowing sleeves gathered in cuffs at the wrist and a plunging neckline. A long silver necklace hung down the middle with a blue stone set in silver hanging at the bottom. Her long, dark hair fell in curls around her shoulders. "It's an honor to have the new Fixer here to support my charity." She ran a red nail down his tie, smiling. Correk looked back at her, bored.

Leira tilted her head to one side, carefully observing the young witch. *I almost think she means it. She's trying to help in her own dangerous dysfunctional way.* "Thank you for thinking of us."

"Come, let me introduce you to a few people. It's a new day and there's no need to let old stories fester and keep us apart anymore. After all, Sirius is gone." Ariana took Leira by the arm, hooking her arm through and walking as if they were old friends finally catching up. Correk arched a brow and followed behind the two women as they walked through the double doors and into the orchestra section of the theater.

Leira couldn't stop herself from looking around the room, her eyes widening. Paintings from Oriceran were hanging in mid-air around the room. Pictures of horses in a field were running back and forth, shaking their manes. A series of paintings with the same garden from different angles had butterflies and ladybugs that appeared in one painting and seemed to fly into another.

A string quartet played on a corner of the stage setting the tone. Tall potted flowers swayed in time with the music.

"Imagine the amount of energy it's taking to keep this

much magic going," said Leira, pulling her arm away. "How are you doing it? There has to be some kind of artifact nearby."

"Good guess, Leira Berens. An old family artifact is strategically placed," said Ariana, with a satisfied smile. She followed Leira's gaze to the simple set up on the stage. "I see you've noticed our prized possession we are auctioning off."

In the center of the stage was a round table with a white tablecloth and a single pewter plate on a stand. A spotlight was focused on it with a small card next to it that read, *'Tudor Reign. Plate of Destiny. Please make a bid.'*

"It's said that King Arthur commissioned the plate from Merlin, a great wizard. His sister married into our family. History never mentions that part. It's been in our family for hundreds of years, locked in a vault. It's about time someone got to enjoy it." Ariana clapped her hands together. "And we can do some good at the same time. Bring the internet to rural areas and to people who are not as fortunate. Everyone wins and we clean out part of our vaults."

"To make room for more." Leira looked up at the plate. "What does that plate do?"

"Oh, that's part of the fun. Buy it and find out."

Leira stared back at her, the two women not saying anything.

Correk came and stood by Leira's side. "Could anyone use a drink?"

"I'm fine," said Ariana, finally turning to smile at a passing guest.

Leira turned around and looked up at the balconies. Each one had small round tables draped in tablecloths with an artifact displayed next to a bid sheet. Handfuls of people were crowded around the tables, peering at the items. Some were writing down their bids. Guards stood at different posts, making sure no one touched an artifact and tried out the magic. Or worse, attempted to steal anything.

Leira narrowed her gaze at the sight of Senator Thatcher in the center of the balcony taking a puff pastry off an offered silver tray. He spotted Leira and held up the hors d'oeuvre before popping it in his mouth.

"He looks like he's having fun," whispered Correk.

"He looks like he's waiting for a root canal," whispered Leira.

"Uncle Felix, have you met Leira?" Ariana held out her arm, waving him toward them. He swirled bourbon in his glass and made no hurry to walk closer.

"Leira Berens, I don't think we've had the pleasure of a formal introduction. Normally, I'm looking at you through smoke and fireballs." He smiled slyly, taking a sip. "And the Fixer. I understand you're obligated to help any magical in trouble, no matter their affiliation. That must put you in an ethical bind every other day."

"That's just you, dear Uncle. Don't project," said Ariana. "Play nice, or else," she added without a hint of a smile. "We're all here to build some new bridges, not settle any scores. Do that on your own time at your own risk," she said, with a threatening look. "Because if I hear about it, you may have need to meet the Fixer again."

Uncle Felix let out a laugh, pressing his hand against his

chest. "I'm so glad you've taken the reins. A breath of fresh air in a very sad and stale family. Where *is* Agnes?" he asked, looking up at the balconies.

"She was unable to attend," said Ariana, scowling at him. Ariana put up a finger. "One moment," she said, gathering her dress and striding over to say hello to another Senator who had just walked in the room. Uncle Felix gave them a nod and a smile as he turned to a group of witches, no longer pretending to be interested.

"Why do I keep hearing the Addams Family theme song in my head." Leira watched Ariana work the room as a waiter came by with a tray of flutes of champagne. Correk took two, handing one to Leira who was looking around the venue. "The only humans here," she said, "are DC bigwigs. Senators mostly. Otherwise it's a mash up of different magicals. When have you ever known the dark families to want to spend time with us common Elf folk?"

"Never. But it's possible that Ariana is trying a new path." Correk sipped the champagne and stopped a waiter passing them with a tray of tiny crab cakes.

"Fuck me, you can't possible think they've decided to turn over a new leaf? That would take a forest as big as the Dark Forest, and just as complicated."

"I think I'm waiting to see what happens. Cautious optimism laced with realism. That was a good crab cake. What else is coming?"

"What does that mean? Not the food, the optimism thing."

"It means I can have a fireball ready in under a second, but I'll wait till it's needed."

"Solid strategy. Let's go look at the silent auction items. See if anything looks particularly radioactive." She took Correk's hand and they started to make their way, stopping every few feet so Correk could sample another tray.

"It's like an upscale Costco on a Saturday," he said, sliding another appetizer into his mouth.

"High praise. You'll have to tell Ariana," said Leira, with a crooked smile.

They finally got to the lobby and were making a turn for the stairs when Leira heard a familiar voice.

"I've always wanted to see the inside of this place. The restoration is said to be amazing. Do you think we'll know anyone here? Oh look, champagne."

"Angel, you're here." Leira went over to hug her neighbor, startling her. But Angel was still quick to return the hug, smiling and talking.

"We're as surprised as you are. I mean, Matt didn't want to come but it's the Howard Theater and an excuse to pull out the really good clothes." She did a pirouette showing off the dark blue, backless dress with long sleeves. "Look at you, Correk. You clean up well." The words poured out of her while Matt stood just behind her, patiently waiting.

"We were just heading upstairs to look at the artifacts," said Leira.

"Oooh, I'm always down for window shopping. Nicole says hello, by the way and we're thinking of trying to go out for dinner, the six of us. You can meet Joe."

Leira and Angel walked toward the stairs as Matt tapped Correk on the arm, slowing him down. "Why do you think the new head of the dark families invited a shifter to her party. A shifter they created for their own dark ends." A flash of anger passed across his face.

"I have no idea yet. All the possibilities are still open. Remember it's Ariana that made a deal with Lucius, your main alpha. She may really want peace." Correk deftly grabbed another crab cake as the tray went by him.

"No one's DNA changes that much, and definitely not that quickly." Matt swallowed hard. "Angel wanted to come so badly, but I don't have a good feeling about it. No one makes up a guest list with powerful magicals and humans and thinks, I need a few shifters in the mix. Not to mention that someone is still poisoning my kind. What if I turn out to be the evening's entertainment?"

"Best advice I can give you is to stay alert and assume nothing." He patted Matt on the back.

"How do you manage to stay so calm?"

"Pretty average day for us," laughed Correk, nodding to Leira who was already heading up the stairs. "This time it even comes with snacks," he said, grabbing a steak and blue cheese bruschetta. "Damn, that was good. Look, Matt, we have to face down darkness all the time. In the hours we're not doing that, we make sure to enjoy and appreciate everything. It's a family rule."

Matt let out a deep breath. "I can try."

"It's all you can ask of yourself."

Correk and Matt wound their way through the crowd milling about in the lobby and headed up the stairs to the mezzanine. A steady stream of magicals and humans were wandering by the line of tables, some occasionally glancing nervously at the beefy magical guards.

Leira stopped at the first table and read the description

out loud. "Teapot from Ming Dynasty. Produces tea that makes the recipient tell the truth for five seconds." There were already a dozen bids on the sheet of paper next to it. "Who would want that? It's like needing to know what will happen next. It's a curse more than a blessing." She looked over the edge of the balcony and saw Lois and Earl swaying to the music together. "Even the Silver Griffins were invited. This is getting odder by the moment."

There was some commotion in the lobby and Leira thought about walking to the stairs but Correk stopped her. "Trouble will find us. Give it a minute. Whoever it is, will come through those doors below," he said, pointing to the crowd below in the orchestra section. "Let's wait up here and see."

The hubbub slowly moved towards the open section below and it wasn't long before Leira and Correk saw who had made a grand entrance. "Wolfstan Humphrey," hissed Leira, the magic suddenly swimming around at her feet, trying to climb up her spine. Symbols flashed on her arms, only to blink off as she tried to suppress the surge of energy.

"Suddenly, this party doesn't seem like such a peace offering." Correk leaned on the railing, his expression cold and resolute.

Leira looked for Ariana in the sea of faces and finally saw her talking to another Senator. She turned when Wolfstan came further into the room and greeted him, pulling him closer to the cluster of politicians. The young witch glanced up at Leira for just a moment, a sly smile on her lips and went back to her conversation, her laughter rising above the general noise.

"I thought the dark families kicked him out," said Correk.

"They did, but maybe not as far as we thought." Leira grew calmer, assessing the situation. "You know, if Hagan were here, he'd be saying to let go of the emotions and add up the clues. The new head of the dark families has invited representatives from almost every power base to mingle in one room. Supposedly, we're supporting her new charity and Ariana is just cleaning out some old artifacts so that everyone benefits. But she's purposely mixed gasoline and matches and seems content with it. That's got motive behind it. The question is, who's her real target. Is it me, is it you? Or is it Wolfstan?"

Correk stood up straighter. "Go on."

"Who stands in her way more? It's not really me, unless she tries to harm someone. If she's just after power, I don't really care. But Wolfstan would care. He'd care a lot and try to steal it from her. She probably looks like easy pickings to him." Leira drank the rest of her champagne. "That girl, though. The waters run very deep and she's playing a game a few steps ahead. No one should ever underestimate a witch who staged a bloodless coup and took over the oldest dark magic on this planet. This night may prove to be more fun than we expected." Leira accepted another glass from a waiter, resting her empty flute on the tray. "Or the dark mist will suddenly appear and try to suck us all in. One of the two."

"Optimistic as always, dear. Now I kind of wish we'd let Yumfuck come with us."

"He'd already be trying to play with the band. I'm not sure the old senators are ready for that."

Wolfstan raised his glass and Leira watched as the others did the same, most with a slight reluctance. She waited for the inevitable and lifted her chin as he turned to look up at the balcony, lifting his glass again to her. She stared at him, taking a sip, keeping her breathing even. *Hagan is right. He's always right.*

CHAPTER FOURTEEN

The night wore on and Leira made sure to know where Wolfstan was in the building, never quite losing sight of him. It wasn't hard. Every time he got within ten feet of her, a swirl of energy ran up her spine, urging her to connect with her magic. An early warning signal.

Leira gratefully listened to Angel describe all the dresses and exclaim over the floating artwork. "We have to find out who catered this party. Maybe they have a shop. That would really dress up our get togethers." It left time for Leira to brush off her old detective skills and keep a watchful eye on everyone and still blend in with the guests. Correk had wandered up to the second level balcony and was inspecting the other artifacts, giving her a wave. She noticed there was a napkin in his other hand piled high with food that he was carefully balancing. "I love him," she muttered, smiling up at him.

"What?" Angel leaned closer. "I couldn't hear you over the noise. This place is jumping. I've never been at a party like this before. Just wait till Norah hears about all of it. We have to have them all over for wine and donuts as soon as possible."

"Wine and donuts. You are my people."

"Well, yeah. I knew that the moment I met you. You're so easy to talk to."

Leira laughed, feeling the tightness between her shoulders easing just a bit. "I'd say the same about you."

Now it was Angel who laughed. "You might want to slow down on the drinking. No one ever says that to me. They'd have to find a way to get a word in first."

"I've never had any trouble," Leira said, squeezing her friend's hand. A photographer passed by, snapping a photo of the two women, quickly moving on to take a picture of Senator Thatcher listening attentively to a man with salt and pepper hair leaning in to make a point. The man turned to get a glass off a tray and the Senator quickly checked his watch. Leira smiled and kept scanning the room.

"That evil man is behaving himself, I see," said Angel, curling her lip.

"You know who Wolfstan Humphrey is?" Leira watched him clapping a wide man in a tight tuxedo on the back, bellowing with laughter.

"Matt told me all about him. They say he's as bad as Sirius."

"That's the first time I've ever heard you say a negative thing about anyone."

"Yeah, well, you really have to earn it. There's a rumor that he's mutilating magicals. Is that true?"

"Let's just say, it's always best to stay away from that Light Elf. Don't even let him learn your name."

"Graaaaaaaa!"

A blood curdling scream tore through the air, startling Angel who sloshed her champagne.

"What the fuck..." muttered Leira, putting her glass on the nearest table and letting the smallest amount of magic finally make its way through her entire body.

Guards stepped forward in front of the tables, shielding the artifacts as aides shuffled some of the Senators toward the exit. The color had drained from Ariana's face, which was twisted in anger. She snapped her fingers at two young wizards who pulled out their wands and went in search of the source of the noise.

Another scream and this time it was closer. The sound brought Lois to the center of the room, near Leira. "Do you think the show has really begun?"

"Hard to say. Can you protect the guests?"

"Already on it." Lois nodded toward Patsy who had out her wand and was getting people to back up and make room.

Leira glanced up at the balcony and saw Correk looking to the far side of the room near a side exit. She followed his line of sight and realized guests were quickly pushing to the left and right, making way for someone. Leira ran toward the corridor that was being formed, the symbols on her arms lighting up and slowly turning. She glanced down and saw it. There's a twist in the plot.

A large, muscular wizard was pushing his way in to the room, his wand drawn and sparking. There was a sheen on his face and his eyes were wild. His shoulder length brown hair was sliding into his eyes and he shoved it back, letting out another scream. That's when Leira saw it poking out from the cuff on his sleeve. His hand was attached to his arm with electronic pieces displaying blinking lights.

Leira spun around till she found Wolfstan who had carefully positioned himself behind a Senator and their aide. Too close for Leira to do anything. She looked back up at the balcony but Correk was gone and when she looked back, he had reappeared behind the wizard.

But before he could do anything, the wizard lashed out, elbowing Correk in the neck and punching a guest in the face. He shook his head, yelling again as Ariana pulled out her wand and yelled a spell in frustration. A pulse of energy swirled in a cyclone, meant to hit only one target. But the wizard raised the artificial arm and swept the cyclone around it, flattening it out and throwing it back at the crowd as if he were bowling. Several magicals fell back in a heap of tangled arms and legs. He raised his arms in the air, making the artificial elements more visible and drawing a gasp from everyone but Wolfstan, Leira and Correk.

Wolfstan stepped around the aide, his eyes glowing and a smile forming at the corners of his mouth.

"No fucking way you're getting credit for this," whispered Leira. She acted quickly, setting an intention. "Help the wizard. Contain him." Energy surged inside of her, pulling her onto her toes and blasting out from the scar on her belly. It shimmered with light, visible to everyone, weaving its way through the room. The Jasper energy swam past Wolfstan who gritted his teeth and held up his hands at waist level trying to cut it off. Blisters appeared on his palms and he flinched, drawing back.

Leira kept her breathing steady, ignoring Wolfstan and

let the energy wrap around the wizard, mingling with his chaotic magic, soothing him. *It's like Peyton.* She recognized the flashes along his energy trail at once. *Wolfstan isn't just replacing parts. He's experimenting with a machine like Harkin's.*

A strand of anger crept into the stream of magic threatening to spread and take over. Her energy did as requested and started to bend in two directions. The wizard began to grimace and let out a howl.

"Focus on who needs your help." Turner Underwood had appeared at her side at just the right moment. He was dressed in his usual suit and wool coat, a bowler placed firmly on his head. "Revenge serves no one and will cause harm eventually. Sometimes in unexpected ways to unintended targets. See the wizard. Help him."

Leira turned her head away from Wolfstan and looked at the wizard.

"See him, feel his confusion and pain. Let the magic wrap him in comfort. Let that be enough for today. It may end up being more than you realize."

Leira let go of the intention to stop Wolfstan, here and now at the gala, and gave control back to the energy. An expansiveness filled her, taking away the anger.

The guests continued to push back against the walls, taking Wolfstan with them. Only Ariana, Correk, Angel and Matt stayed in the center of the room with Leira. Patsy and Lois were just in front of the crowd, making sure the wizard didn't suddenly turn on them.

Senator Thatcher pushed his way past his aide and stood at the edge of the crowd, intently watching Leira work. It was the first time all night he looked engaged and like he was glad he was there.

Wolfstan noticed too and growled, holding out his injured hands as a waiter brought him ice wrapped in a cloth napkin.

Leira kept the energy steady as Correk moved closer, practicing the spells Turner had taught him. But it wasn't quite enough and Correk knew it. He looked across the room to his mentor who gave him a nod. Correk created a ball of light in his hands and gently tossed it in the air above them. A shadow came over the crowd, making everything indistinct.

When it cleared, Correk and the wizard were gone. Leira felt the magic returning to her, sliding back down her spine.

Turner Underwood tapped the brim of his hat with his cane. "I'm afraid I need to get back to my dinner companion. Never leave a beautiful woman alone for too long."

"I'll be sure to tell Correk."

Turner chuckled and made his way into the crowd, disappearing somewhere in the middle.

"It's like magic Uber," muttered Leira. She looked around for Wolfstan Humphrey, but he was gone as well. Leira clenched her fists and thought about following his trail. "This has to end."

"Don't be so sure the end isn't already playing out." Ariana came and stood next to her, her wand still in her hand. "That was some impressive use of magic. I don't think I've ever seen that kind of finesse before and I've seen some of the best who don't care about rules."

"Thank you, sort of. I need to go."

"Don't be in such a hurry. Let Wolfstan go this time." She smiled, this time letting it reach her eyes. She turned around and glanced up at the stage. Leira saw it at once.

"The plate is gone." She tilted her head and looked at Ariana. "I wondered why all the muscle was in the balcony. I'm surprised Wolfstan fell for it."

"Oh, there was a pretty powerful ward around it that would have kept out almost everyone. I had to make it a little hard for him."

"Be careful when you're playing with Wolfstan. I wouldn't be so sure that he can't take anything and make it into a cruel asset for himself.

Ariana tapped Leira on the shoulder with her wand, sending a low vibration of magic through the Jasper Elf. "You and I should talk sometime. This feud benefits no one."

"I was never feuding, Ariana. That's all on you."

"Even better," she said, waving her wand in the air. "I'll be in touch." The young witch turned and waved her wand, amplifying her voice. "Everyone, the commotion has subsided and there is still work to be done for the less fortunate." She waved to the waiters to go back among the crowd, passing out drinks and circulating the food. "Eat, drink and keep bidding and save up your stories for your friends." She leaned toward one of the guards and whispered, "Remove the table on the stage and replace it with flowers." The music resumed and several of the guests headed for the door, but most stayed.

Leira made her way to the door, waiting till she could find a dark spot on the street to open a portal.

"That was quite impressive." Senator Thatcher stepped

out from a throng of people. "I was right about you. I'm glad you're our first bounty hunter. You will set an example that will be difficult to match, which is what you want. A high bar."

"I didn't stop the real cause of the problem."

"You think it was Wolfstan Humphrey's doing, don't you? I saw the way you looked at him."

"He's a monster beyond all others. Be very careful around him. Don't let him get too close."

The Senator's face twitched but he said nothing. Leira noticed and gave him a nod. "You know where to find me. Just don't wait too long."

Leira made her way out of the theater and turned the corner to the side of the building and a dark, empty lot. Angel and Matt came running around the corner after her, holding hands. "Are you okay?" exclaimed Angel, just as Leira was about to create a ball of light.

"I'm fine, just tired. I'm going to call it a night."

"Out here? This isn't the way home," said Angel, looking back in the direction of N Street.

Leira smiled and said, "Let's go home a different route tonight. Just this once." She opened her hand as a ball of purple light began to grow in her palm. She pulled it apart as Angel and Matt watched in wonder. A portal opened to Leira's kitchen just as the troll looked back and jumped off the counter, running for the stairs. "That's going to be an interesting conversation," said Leira. "Come on, you can go through first, Angel. Then you, Matt."

Angel clapped her hands, her eyes still wide. She gingerly stepped through, still holding hands with Matt as he followed closely behind her. "Can you imagine if you could do this, Matt? We could get to work in seconds. Can these things take you anywhere? What else can you do?"

Leira snorted with laughter and stepped through just as a thud sounded over her head from Yumfuck's room. "I am going to figure that out," she muttered, letting the portal close, sparks dancing around the kitchen floor.

"Now that was a party," said Angel. "It had everything. Magic, good food, bubbly, danger, intrigue and good friends."

"That's one way to look at it," said Leira, taking off her shoes. She opened the fridge and leaned in to get a beer. "Anyone want a beer?"

"An after party. We are getting cooler," said Angel, taking a beer and passing it to Matt.

"Are you sure we're not keeping you up?" asked Matt.

"Not at all. This is kind of an Austin tradition for me, except there was a bar right outside my door. It just makes it all feel a little more like home."

CHAPTER FIFTEEN

Peyton sat outside the small cafe drinking an espresso. He was still getting used to being back in any world, even if it was set up as New York City from a long time ago.

"Is this seat taken?" Cari smiled, pulling out the metal chair next to Peyton. "Travi will be along shortly. She will be so glad we got to see you."

"Travi is the bright spot in any day." Peyton swirled the remains of his espresso in the cup, a spark of magic jolting through his body, making his bones ache.

"Is it still happening?" Cari held up her hand, shaking her head. "It's none of my business, I'm sorry. I shouldn't intrude."

Peyton's eyebrows went up and he reached out for Cari's hand. "You could never intrude. Yes, it's still happening, but it's manageable. And if I compare it to where I was not too long ago, this is nothing. I have my sanity back. I can live without magic, if I have to."

"You haven't lost your magic."

"No, but I also can't be sure that I can control it. It's almost the same. Hell, I'm not even sure what I can do anymore. Turner Underwood said that will be our next big adventure."

"Then there's hope. Maybe you will find some new and exciting abilities. Like that Spider Man. Travi loves that story. A boy who is changed forever with almost no family, but still he persists."

Peyton took a longer look at Cari. "But can you live without more freedom? I mean, this is paradise," he said, looking around at the townhouses and shops along the busy street. "But unless you know you can leave, it's just a velvet prison."

"It's safe and Travi can grow here..." Her words trailed off.

"You are a terrible liar. One of your many wonderful qualities."

Cari gave a pained smile and ducked her chin.

"I want to do something to help. To help all of you. Winland Underwood found the traitor, but no one has been able to draw him out again."

"We'll find him. He can't hide from an entire world of magicals. We'll get him," she said, not sounding too confident.

"Travi!" Peyton called out to the young Elven girl as she came running across the street. Too late, a Model T came barreling down the road at Travi. The young Elf froze, staring at the car as the driver hit the brakes. Peyton stood up, knocking over the chair and threw out his hands without thinking, his eyes taking on an amber glow. The ground in front of Travi curled into the air acting as a barrier and stopping the car just in time. Cari ran to her daughter pulling her close. "Are you alright? You have to remember to look for horses and cars!"

Travi was staring at the curled ground and back at Peyton. A smile grew on her face, her hand pressed against her chest. "That was so cool. How did you do that? I didn't even see you use a spell or move your fingers or make a ball of light. You are awesome!"

Cari turned and looked at the wave of dirt and pavers, perfectly curled against the car. Several other magicals had also gathered and were looking at the phenomenon from every angle. The driver had even finally gotten out of his car and was looking at the bumper. "Nothing is even dented!" he exclaimed, throwing up his hands, his mouth hanging open. "How did you do that?"

"I... I don't even know. I didn't have time to think about it. I just knew what I wanted to happen."

Travi ran to Peyton and tugged on his arm. "Do something else. Can you make the ground curl back down?" Travi looked at her mother but Cari shrugged, waiting for Peyton to answer.

"I have no idea."

"Well," said Cari, "how did you feel when you managed to do that?"

"I don't know, panicked," said Peyton, righting the chair and walking out to the curb.

"No, you weren't panicked. You were determined. You stopped thinking and wondering and just acted." Cari came and stood next to him, looking at the car. The wizard driving it used his wand to move the car, leaving the curl of dirt as a strange sculpture in the middle of the road. "Maybe years of thinking when you were trapped inside your own body are getting in your way. What if you just tried doing what you want to do? What you really want to do. Just do it," said Cari, snapping her fingers. "Don't think about it."

Peyton impulsively grabbed Cari's hand and kissed her lightly on the lips, surprising both of them. Cari felt the pulse of magic pass between them. She stiffened at first but relented and put her hands on either side of his face, kissing him back.

Travi jumped up and down, clapping her hands. "Oooooh, that's a kind of magic!" She picked up a glass of water, still excited and started to take a sip, splashing the contents.

But instead of hitting the front of her blouse, the water rolled backward, floating in droplets just above the glass. Travi looked down at the glass and up at Peyton. "You did it again!" Travi moved the glass around, delighted that the droplets followed her motions.

Cari smiled gently and stood in front of Peyton. "How are you feeling right this moment? Magic runs on feelings. Tune into it, recognize what it feels like and where it came from."

Peyton closed his eyes. A crowd was gathering while magicals were darting off to find others to tell. People were leaning out their windows, watching the spectacle. Winland Underwood came up on the crowd and made her way to the front.

"Okay, good," said Cari. "Now take in a deep breath and let that feeling settle inside of you. Let go of all the sounds out here except for my voice." She slowly waved a hand to Travi to hold very still, the droplets still floating above the glass.

"I know you can still feel it. The magic is still emanating off you." She bit her lip and held her breath.

"It feels like... like nothing. Like no troubles or worries or thoughts. It's just there. If I think about it too much, it seems to melt away."

Cari watched the droplets dip down toward the glass and the dirt start to curl back into place.

"Then let go. You trust me, I know you do. Trust that feeling and let it be there with you."

The droplets rose again and twirled in a circle as if they were on a carousel. Travi slapped a hand over her mouth trying not to giggle.

"See if you can increase the feeling and set it loose, just a little."

The electric streetlights flickered on and then off, and then on again, flashing up and down the street. Cari looked back and forth at the street, the droplets and the lights.

"How is this possible?" whispered Winland.

Cari clasped her hands together and slowly asked Peyton another question. "Peyton, can you let that feeling root inside of you *and* think about the air around me at the same time? Just try it. No attachment to what might happen." Air began to blow up from the street, filling Cari's wide skirt like a cloth balloon. She smiled broadly, pushing down on it, her eyes wide with wonder. "Okay, now try releasing the energy slowly. Just let it float away and dissipate."

One by one the droplets fell back into the glass. The street curled back into place. The lights flickered off and stayed that way, and her skirt flattened back down. "Open your eyes, Peyton." She took his hand and held it between hers, waiting till he was looking at her. "I think I know what magic you possess and it's the rarest of its kind. You can manipulate elements. Air, earth, water. Probably even fire. It's amazing," she said in a hushed voice.

"I knew it! You are wonderful! You're a superhero!" Travi sloshed the water down her dress at last and leaped forward, hugging Peyton around the waist.

"She's right," said Cari, "but I knew that before anything happened."

Winland walked around the magicals still marveling over the place in the street that was curved just moments ago. She came and stood next to Travi, peering down in the glass and cleared her throat. "Peyton, I have something I want to try. Do you think you'd be game?"

He sputtered and started to say no, but Winland interrupted him. "It may help us catch the traitor and set all of us free. You may actually be the key."

Peyton looked at Cari and at Travi's beaming face. "Then how could I say no? What is it?"

"Okay, repeat the exercise Cari tried with you, only this time direct the energy. Direct the electricity, into this device." Winland tried to hide her excitement as she held up a cell phone and then placed it on the table in front of Peyton. Cari nodded to him, her lips pressed together.

"Why is he here?" Peyton looked up from the wingback upholstered chair at Cousin Petie's waxed moustache and his lanky frame in the worn tuxedo.

"Hey dude, I'm just here to help. I came out of a very safe nest to try and catch this bastard."

"Cousin Petie is one of us," said Winland. 'Not only that, he's saved more of us over the years than we can count. Plus, he has a lot of connections out there."

They were sitting in her father's parlor with the curtains drawn, away from prying eyes. "No pressure. It's just an idea I had and if it doesn't work, we'll come up with a different idea."

"No pressure. Good to know," Peyton grumbled, eliciting a chortle from Cari.

"Peyton, you've come a long way in a short amount of time. We're all just glad that you're doing so well. This part is gravy," said Cari. "Breathe with me and let's get back that feeling of connection to something inside of you." Cari took in an exaggerated deep breath, holding it for a moment and then letting it back out. "Remember what you learned as a small child on Oriceran. Magic is always about feelings. Thinking tends to get in the way. The mind is only there to focus the energy, but not to demand."

Peyton shook out his hands and looked up at the row of eager faces. "Maybe if everyone backs up a little. Who had pizza already today?"

"Oooh, my bad," said Cousin Petie, holding a hand covered in rings up to his mouth. He took a step back along with Winland and Cari and everyone waited.

Peyton looked at them again and shook his head, closing his eyes. "I never have liked pizza," he muttered. "Okay, let everything go. It's not like it hasn't been a hundred years or more since I've directed anything." He centered himself and felt just enough of the same spark deep inside to get him started. He let the same feeling of contentment without end spread across his belly.

"Give a simple direction." Cari's voice echoed in his head. The magic was already growing and the ache in his bones was easing. He opened his eyes and reached out for the phone, grasping it in his hands.

Winland stifled a gasp as Cousin Petie twirled the end of his moustache and muttered softly, "Oh my. Abracadabra indeed."

Peyton's eyes were glowing a steady green and miniature sparks of electricity danced across them.

Cari took Winland's hand and held it tight. "He's doing it."

Sparks jumped from his skin, riding up and down his arms. Winland held her breath, staring at the phone. Suddenly the screen came on and she startled, squeezing Cari's hand in surprise. She nodded to Cari, "Give him the instructions, just like we practiced."

"Okay Peyton, send the signal out in search of Erickson. Use the connection we set up to the first security cameras and let the magic do the work."

"You really think this can work?" Cousin Petie smacked his lips together nervously.

Peyton's body relaxed and his shoulders dropped. He became unaware of the room he was in or the people around him as he followed the thread of magic, watching as pictures began to emerge.

"Give it a second," said Winland. "Wait... wait... look! It's working!"

Images began to scroll across the face of the phone showing different angles of streets and alleys as the magic searched for Erickson.

"He's a marvel," said Cousin Petie breathlessly.

The pictures from different cameras kept appearing, picking up speed till they were just a blur. At last, the images began to slow and ticked over, one at a time till it came to rest.

Winland took in a sharp intake of breath. "We have him! There he is."

Erickson could be seen walking across a city street, pulling a coat close around his shoulders, his head down.

Winland quickly checked the coordinates of the camera, looking over Peyton's shoulder at the phone in his hand. "He's in Cleveland." She jerked her head up abruptly. "We need to tell my father. Now. Erickson's hunting more refugees."

Winland opened up her hand, a dozen golden fireballs no bigger than a pea bobbled about in her palm. Each one had a protrusion poking out that kept jabbing at her hand. "They're nuisance balls. This will get his attention." She threw them up into the air and watched them careen toward the walls, melting into them and reappearing on the other side. The sped off, streaks of light seeking out the old Fixer.

"Phones don't work for the Fixer?" asked Cari.

"My father could be on another world or another plane

or on a date with his phone turned off," she said, her hands on her hips with a wink. "But we have an agreement that I don't send those unless it's an emergency."

"Look!" Cari pointed at the screen. Erickson was staring right back at them and pointing his wand in the direction of the camera. Passerby were glancing back at him with curious looks.

"Magic in broad daylight no less," said Cousin Petie. "My how the mighty have fallen."

Erickson flicked his wand forward, his arms outstretched. A sudden flash lit up the phone, fading into darkness. Peyton jerked back to reality, the ache returning to his joints. His eyes popped open, the green iridescent glow gone.

"Was that enough?" he asked. "Did it work?"

"Like a charm," smiled Cari, kissing him on his forehead.

"You, my friend, are a one-of-a-kind magical. A Light Elf who is also an Elementor." Cousin Petie twirled the end of his moustache. "A regular marvel! You will always be welcomed at the Carnival Lounge."

Peyton looked at Cari, confused. "That's a good thing," said Cari, smiling.

"Where's Turner Underwood? I thought he'd be here by now." Peyton sat up, stretching his tight back.

"My father always has a unique way of doing things. Give it a second."

Poof.

A dark cloud erupted in the center of a side table, evaporating to reveal a cream-colored card. Written on it in calligraphy was, *I'm on it. Love, Dad.*

"Your childhood must have been amazing."

Winland and Cari turned to look at Cousin Petie. "Look where we're standing. I'm a refugee in a make believe world. It had a few hiccups." She looked down at the note. "But it had a lot of good times too."

CHAPTER SIXTEEN

Leira wandered down the stairs early in the morning in her bare feet, still dressed in pajamas. She paused at the first floor landing, biting her lip. Yumfuck's door was slightly ajar. "Don't do it," she muttered, even as her feet were tiptoeing in that direction. "I *should* let it be. Turn back now." She put out her hand to gently push the door.

A tiny furry face appeared in the crack at the bottom of the door. "Can I help you?" asked the troll, pulling the door closer to his head.

Leira stopped abruptly looking down at the five inch figure squeezed in the opening. "I was stopping by to say hello. You know, I've been thinking it's been a while since we've sat down and talked." She shrugged, puckering her lips. "I thought maybe I'd come in for a few minutes, sit on your bed, catch up on how you've been doing..."

"Life's been good, no complaints," said Yumfuck, not budging. "Some pretty good bed head you got going there. Good party last night?"

"It was the usual with a brief battle." Leira patted down

her hair. "Anything interesting going on?"

"Not so much. You?"

Leira eyed him suspiciously. The troll responded with a smile, showing all his tiny teeth.

"I'm good too. You sure you don't want to hang for a little bit?"

"No, I have a pretty packed day. You making pancakes? I want mine with chocolate chips."

Leira leaned to the right hoping to get even a sliver of a glance but everything looked normal from the three inch view that was visible.

"Why would I make pancakes? It's a workday and you already said you're busy."

"Hmph, I'd have thought you'd treat your mother better than that."

Leira stopped trying to get a peek and looked down at the troll. "My mother? What does my mother have to do with pancakes?"

"She's in the kitchen waiting for you."

Leira adjusted her faded Jon Bon Jovi t-shirt that worked as a pajama top. "My mom is in the kitchen and you didn't say anything?"

"She said not to wake you up. If you make the pancakes, remember the chocolate chips." The door shut with a sharp click before Leira could say anything else. "Next time!" She headed for the stairs, running down them and leaping off the last few to the foyer, dashing down the hall. She got to the kitchen and sitting quietly at the table was Eireka Entin, sipping a cup of tea.

"Mom! What are you doing here?"

"Nice way to greet your mother." Eireka smiled, arching

a brow.

Leira did her best to quickly recover and smiled, leaning over to hug Eireka. "I mean, what a great surprise. Your first visit... and no warning." Leira glanced toward the dishes in the sink. Correk came in the back door with a white paper bag. "Oh, you're up. I got muffins for everyone. The good donuts were already gone."

"You knew Mom was here?" said Leira, trying to give him a look.

Correk shrugged and put the bag down, leaning sideways to give Leira a kiss. "Your mom said not to wake you."

"Next time, wake me," she whispered in his ear.

Eireka opened the bag, smiling and pulled out a blueberry muffin.

"Mom, why are you here? How did you even get here? You aren't big on portal jumping."

"I took the train," she said, holding up her Starbucks cup. "It took no time at all and I got the chance to walk through your neighborhood. This area is lovely! Did you know you have an entire building of magicals right down the street?"

"Yumfuck already scoped them out." Leira put one hand back on her hip, leaning on the table. "Are you really going to make me ask you a third time?"

Eireka tilted her head to the side and looked at her only child. "I'm your mother and I haven't seen you in person in months. That's it, no other reason."

"You know, I have somewhere I need to be," said Correk, reaching into the bag and pulling out a carrot muffin as he scooted down the hallway.

"That's a carrot one. You're not gonna like it as much as

you think you will." Eireka gave him a crooked smile watching him bite into it. He shrugged and turned for the stairs. "It has pineapple and raisins. I'll make do."

"Come sit by me." Eireka patted the chair next to her. Leira sat down and Eireka brushed a lock of her daughter's hair behind her ear, smiling. "You are a remarkable woman, even without all the magic."

"You're really freaking me out here, Mom."

"You'll understand someday. You and Correk will have a child and watch them grow and know where they are all the time. Then one day, they'll decide to go fight monsters and you'll be happy for them, but it won't be the same."

"Kid of our own," said Leira, her eyes growing wider. "Can you imagine? Who would babysit a tiny magical for us when we run off to fight the bad guys? Yumfuck?"

"I've heard worse ideas. And there's me, you know. I might even give in to a portal or two for that kind of reason. I could back up Yumfuck."

"I think Yumfuck's building something in his room, but he won't tell me what it is." Leira narrowed her eyes, tilting her head. "Do trolls have any weird powers I don't know about yet?"

Eireka let out a snort of laughter. "No, you've pretty much seen the range that I know about." Eireka put her arm around Leira and pulled her closer. "Tell me you've figured out how to best Wolfstan Humphrey."

Leira pulled away just far enough to see her mother's face. "Is that why you're here? You're really worried this time. That's saying something."

"I've been really worried before. I haven't forgotten the battle with Rhazdon." She let out a sigh. "But then I could see you all the time. Now I have to send out a little magic to check on you and hope. It's the longest minute of my day. Wolfstan may actually be more dangerous than Rhazdon."

"Hard to say. Rhazdon had a pretty good run of evil." Leira leaned her head on her mother's shoulder. "What if I come to visit more often? And when that idea blows up in my face because of bounty hunter duties, what if I fill in with at least letting you know every night that we're all safe and sound."

Eireka kissed the top of Leira's head, breathing in the scent of her hair. "I will take that deal and I'll make a point of visiting you more often too."

"You want to meet the neighbors?" Leira sat up, excited. "You'll love her. Her name is Angel and she knows a lot about the city. We can get her to take us on a walk."

Eireka's eyes shined and she blinked away a tear. "I don't think I've ever seen you this happy. Not ever. You are blossoming here. I think that's what I really needed to know. Sure, let's go meet Angel and take a long walk."

Leira got up to go change and was almost to the stairs.

"Oh, by the way, Yumfuck showed me what he's doing in his room," said Eireka, laughing as she took another sip of her tea. She put down her cup and ran her pinched fingers along her lips. "I'm not saying a word. He'll tell you when he's ready. It's good practice for when you have kids."

Leira started up the stairs. "You're really on this kid thing today."

"When you're ready, of course," her mother called out.

"When I'm ready," muttered Leira. "When would that be?"

CHAPTER SEVENTEEN

"Everything you said about Angel is true. I like her." Eireka and Leira were walking the short distance back to the townhouse.

"She's kind of like everyone at the bar rolled into one person."

"Except for Estelle." Eireka took Leira's hand to pass through the wards.

"Goes without saying. Estelle is definitely one of a kind. Hug her for me, next time you see her. How did you get past the wards the first time? It was the troll, wasn't it? Small but clever." Leira walked in the front door with her mother and heard laughter coming from the kitchen. "Who keeps getting past all the wards?"

"I'd know one of those voices anywhere," said Eireka. "You must have put out a wish of your own." Eireka nudged her daughter down the hallway. "Go see your father. From the sounds of it, he brought a friend."

"Dad's here!" Leira dropped her purse in the nearest chair and took off running down the hall. She found

Jackson sitting at the kitchen table playing cards with Yumfuck. A purple-haired troll was sitting near her father's arm, holding up three cards.

"Three Dark Forests and a Double Moon. Read em and weep," said Yumfuck, pushing all the Cheetos toward his side of the table. He split off a third of them and slid them toward the other troll. "A welcome present."

Leira hugged her father around his neck, squeezing tight.

"Hey, that's a greeting," said Jackson, throwing down his cards. "Eireka?" He looked past Leira at Eireka standing in the doorway and alarm grew in his voice. "Is everything okay?"

"Everything is fine. I just missed my daughter," said Eireka coming all the way in and taking a seat near Yumfuck. "Look at this, Leira has both her parents in the same room." She reached out to scoop up the other troll. "And who are you, little fella? Yumfuck did you make a friend in the neighborhood."

Leira smiled, watching her father shift uncomfortably in his seat. "Tell her, Dad. Tell Mom she no longer has to worry about you living alone in that cabin in the woods."

"I'm not alone. There's my dog."

"What?" Eireka watched the troll climb up her arm and take a seat on her shoulder. He was holding a Cheetos in his paws, nibbling on the top. "You're definitely not related to Yumfuck. Wait, is this *your* troll, Jackson? You bonded with a troll?" Eireka's smile grew, deepening her dimples as her forehead wrinkled. "I thought you knew how to avoid rescuing a troll," she said, grinning.

"I still do, but daughters have proven to be a lot trickier."

"Dad rescued a troll that had been sheared from its magical. He's a hero," said Leira, eating a Cheetos.

"I'm a hero," said Jackson, his face warming.

"Wooooowwww! And you fell for that one," said Eireka.

"It meant a lot to Leira and she said it made up for over twenty something missed birthdays." Jackson looked sheepish, spreading his hands out on the table.

"I suppose you had that one coming." Eireka put the troll back on the table.

"For the umpteenth time I didn't know I had a daughter."

"Ancient History," interrupted Leira.

"And now you have a tiny warrior by your side. What's his name?" Eireka pursed her lips, trying not to laugh.

"You are enjoying this even more than I expected." Jackson gave the same lopsided grin as his daughter. "Nibbler. I mean, look at him," said Jackson, leaning across the table to rub the top of the troll's head. "He's still working on the same Cheetos. He'll be at it for a few minutes." The troll looked up and smiled at Jackson, who smiled back at him.

"Dad, I think you actually like the little guy."

"He's alright and he gets along with my dog."

"Very basic requirements."

Yumfuck picked up a Cheetos and opened his mouth wide, pushing it in and chomping as fast as he could till it was gone. He picked up another and repeated the process, working his way through the pile.

"It's like everyone mysteriously got the troll that was right for them," said Eireka, amused.

"Not sure how to take that. I don't eat that fast, do I?" Leira looked at Yumfuck and back at her orange fingers.

"Have you ever let coffee cool off before you slurp it?" asked Eireka.

"Have you ever let the cheese cool on a pizza?" asked her father.

"Okay, okay, I get it. I'm enthusiastic about food and Dad is kind of mellow. That is weird."

Yumfuck looked up at the clock on the wall. "I gotta go see a guy. Hey, Nibbler, you want to go with me?"

Nibbler looked to Jackson for approval.

"It's fine with me, but keep an eye on him, Yumfuck. He's not used to the city."

"Aw, that's sweet. Dad's making sure his troll stays safe." Leira picked up Yumfuck and held him in front of her face. "No crime fighting as long as Nibbler's along, no underground trains, and no weird schemes. You and I both know what I mean."

Yumfuck nodded his head. "Deal."

"Uncross your paws and say that again."

Yumfuck let out an exasperated sigh and held up his paws. "Still a deal. Come on Nibbler, let's blow this joint. We'll be back by the time the streetlights are on, maybe sooner." Yumfuck waited for Nibbler to scurry down Eireka's arm and took him by the paw as they worked their way off the table. Leira opened the back door and pointed two fingers at Yumfuck and back at her eyes. "I meant what I said. You're the senior statesman. Take good care of him."

"I wouldn't let anything happen to him. He's my new buddy. Enjoy Parents Day. Show them your cubby."

"Funny, troll." She watched them scamper down the back steps and disappear around the side of the building. "Why do I worry? They can grow to eight feet and take out a bad guy with one swipe."

Yumfuck and Nibbler sat side by side on the bench in the park waiting patiently for Samuel Akins. It wasn't long before Yumfuck heard the familiar tap-tap of Samuel's cane coming down the path.

"Hellooooo!" Yumfuck stood up on the bench, putting his paws around his mouth and calling to his friend.

"Hello to you." Samuel found his way to his usual spot on the bench and eased himself down, propping his cane between his legs. "How is everything on your side of the street today?"

"A pretty okay day. I have a new friend. Meet Nibbler. We helped save him from extermination."

Nibbler waved a paw, grinning.

"What's happening? Is he saying something?" Samuel put out his hand, waiting.

Yumfuck rolled his eyes and slapped his face with his paw. "He's not much for talking, but he'll catch on."

Samuel's brow furrowed. "Another troll? This is a good day." Samuel put his hand down, laying it flat against the bench. Yumfuck nudged Nibbler toward the elderly man.

The slightly smaller troll crawled into Samuel's palm

and trilled as Samuel picked him and held him close, stroking his soft head.

"You are a good friend, Yumfuck. You saved a friend and you helped me heal broken parts of myself that I had resigned myself to believing would always bear a wound." Samuel turned his face to the sun. "Nice weather, good friends. It is a pretty okay day. How could this day get any better?"

"Donuts would help," said Yumfuck. "Donuts can improve anything."

Samuel snorted with laughter, jiggling Nibbler.

"Donuts," squeaked Nibbler.

"He speaks! Well, then we have to get some to make this a perfect day. They're on me today, too," said Samuel, slapping a knee. "A perfect day."

"You're easy to please, Samuel. I like that about you." Yumfuck dropped down to the ground and waited for Nibbler, taking his paw. They walked next to Samuel in the direction of the donut shop, just enjoying the day.

CHAPTER EIGHTEEN

The Willen ran down the crooked street, past the faded wooden sign that read, *Fairhaven Kemana. Welcome.*

He was panting hard, running on all four away from the town square and toward the darker streets. In this part of town, the light was purposely dimmed even during the day as a nod to the Willens who lived there.

The brass buttons on the Willen's velvet vest clinked along the uneven cobblestones. He glanced back over his shoulder, his eyes wide with panic and fear.

"I'll find you!" A booming voice echoed off the houses. The sound enhanced by magic. Wolfstan Humphrey came running down the road, his eyes glowing and a fireball already formed in his hand. He was dressed in his old Oriceran clothes, a long jacket hanging over suede pants and tall boots with buckles.

"Ollie, ollie oxen free!" he bellowed to pull the Willen out of hiding. "Give me the ring," he yelled, "and you can go on your way. Don't give it to me and you may not like the ending. I'm in need of a few more test subjects. Rats are infamous for being great in that line of work."

The Willen felt the pull of the spell and held onto the dented downspout of the house, but his paws were slipping. "No, I can't...," he said, the strain in his voice. Inside his jacket, in the innermost pocket sat a small box with a signet ring inside. "It was entrusted to me," said the Willen, digging his claws into the metal. He lifted his chin just enough to pucker and released a mournful whistle. The Willen sucked in more air and did it again.

Wolfstan stopped running and stood in the middle of the street, looking around at all the houses. Each one was slightly broken down with a broken step or a cracked window or a few missing tiles on the roof. But in each window could still be seen a warm glow, sometimes filtered through a torn lace curtain.

"I would hate to see anything happen to your friends and neighbors." Wolfstan formed a fireball and threw it down the center of the street, leaving a burning trail that cast a glow against all the houses, reflecting in the windows. "No? Okay, have it your way, but I tried," he growled.

The Light Elf's lip curled in disgust. "How about this nice pile of wood some rat family is calling home?" Wolfstan grew another large fireball in his right hand and walked closer to a blue bungalow with a small bike propped against the porch. "Last chance... Ollie ollie oxen free."

The sound of scratching could be heard coming from more than one direction. Wolfstan hesitated, looking up and down the street, but nothing seemed to be moving in the shadows. He shrugged and leaned back to throw the fireball. But an unexpected sharp pain in his ankle stopped him. His hand wobbled as he looked down, but he saw nothing. He pulled his arm back again and started to heave but there was another sharp pain, this time in his other ankle. And this time, he dropped the fireball, singeing his own foot. "Son of a damn rat!"

The artificial light overhead darkened further making it difficult to see along the streets. The other parts of Fairhaven could be seen in the lights in the distance.

Wolfstan turned in a circle, looking around at the houses. All of the lights in the windows had also gone out. He chortled loudly. "Very clever rats, but it won't change a thing." He threw a ball of light over his head illuminating the area right around him and stretching in degrees a few feet further.

A dark, undulating wave of fur seemed to be taking shape just outside the glimmer.

"What now?" he yelled.

A round piece of metal zinged through the air, piercing the ball of light and snuffing it out, throwing Wolfstan back into obscurity. Anger crawled up his spine, leaving a ringing in his ears. "Not this week!" he yelled. "I've already had enough this week. Did you hear me? Enough!" He quickly made another fireball and wasted no time leaning back to throw it. This time he felt the pressure of sharp teeth from both sides biting down hard, managing to pierce his boots. Searing pain shook his bones and the fireball once again slid off the back of his hand. The different sets of teeth relented, pulling back. The tip of a pink tale could be seen slipping away from the flash of light.

MARTHA CARR & MICHAEL ANDERLE

Wolfstan raised his fists in anger, lifting his chin to roar into the darkness. "I will have that ring!" He crossed his arms over his head, summoning all his energy and swept them apart yelling, "Omnes Orbem Accensum." Light from above filled the neighborhood, filling in the shapes of every corner, of every house, and every patch of ground.

Just for a moment, Wolfstan smiled in delight that something was finally working out for him. But that was as long as it lasted. As he turned away from the lights of Fairhaven, he saw the same undulating wave of dark fur. His brow furrowed for a second as he realized it was hundreds of Willens, whisker to whisker.

They were packed together in rows, down on their paws and staring at Wolfstan, their fangs bared. Wolfstan felt a brief pang of worry, an unusual feeling. It was making him just a little slow to react. He opened his mouth and uttered, "Ignis..." but got no further.

Shoppers in the town square in the distance looked up from their tables at the sudden sound of hundreds of claws skittering across pavement and squeals from hundreds of Willens. One or two even peeked down the side street that lead to the center of the Willen's village, but no one took a step in that direction.

The Willens advanced as one large moving unit, easily taking over Wolfstan and pulling him down before he could finish the spell. "Not a rat," yelled a large Willen, standing on his chest. "Willens!"

They bit at his flesh and tore off anything shiny from his clothes, shredding his jacket and ripping his boots. But Wolfstan wasn't ready to give up without a fight. He threw out small fireballs from his badly injured hand, pushing open a space large enough to give himself some room. He kept pelting the Willens, falling to one knee as he hastily made a ball of light in one hand, whispering into it to make it wider and create a portal. On the other side was his office high over a Washington Street. The walls of the portal quivered, making a few of the closest Willens pull back.

"It's unstable!" yelled a female Willen in an old yellow satin dress.

Wolfstan looked at the shaking portal and back at the sea of Willens. He fell backward into the portal, the upper half of his body landing safely on his thick office carpet. But a tear in the bottom of the portal pulled even wider and hands reached out from the world in between, grabbing onto his already battered legs. His backside slid a few inches across the carpet as most of the Willens gasped. A thin, red haired Willen was still stowing away a few shiny buttons in the fold of his skin.

"Igni summam." Wolfstan choked out the words, willing himself not to fall unconscious from the pain. A blue flame circled his legs burning the hands that reached out for him and further destroying his boots. The hands fell away, letting Wolfstan pull himself the rest of the way into his office, letting the portal close with a loud hiss. The high-pitched sound of a hundred screaming voices could be heard till the very last second.

Wolfstan rolled over and rested his head against the carpet. "The time is drawing near to make everyone listen," he barked.

The sound of his assistant's footsteps could be heard coming down the hall. He burst into the office and drew back, his eyes wide at the sight of a bloodied and torn Wolfstan Humphrey laying back on the carpet. "I'll... I'll get help," said the young man, dropping his folder and running back down the hall yelling for help as he dialed his phone.

"Soon, soon." The words slipped out of his mouth as he closed his eyes and darkness returned.

The Willens dispersed back to their houses and the lights went back to their more normal dusk. A larger Willen in a shiny red jacket embroidered in gold and threadbare at the elbows ran into his house, leaving the door open. It took him a minute to find a piece of paper and a leaky pen and scribble, '*The ring is safe and has been moved again. Wolfstan is badly injured. Maybe a little angry. He got away. Be careful.*' He came back out, scurrying down the stairs with a note and handed it to a younger Willen who had been waiting, whiskers twitching.

"Give this to your cousin, Vinnie and use the southwest network to move the message to Washington DC. It's got to get to Leira Berens as fast as possible." The younger Willen nodded and put the note into the folds of his skin, adjusting a few metal pieces that jangled and clinked unseen and safely tucked away. He hugged the older Willen and took off running on all fours for the exit from the Fairhaven kemana to start the relay chain and warn Leira Berens. Wolfstan Humphrey was a growing danger.

CHAPTER NINETEEN

Leira stood in front of the Georgian style mansion on Massachusetts Avenue set near the Estonian embassy. She had been standing in front of the tall gate for over a minute getting her mind set for entering a house owned by the Dark Family. "I am volunteering to go inside the front door in broad daylight. My, how times have changed." Her phone binged and she looked down at the text. "How does that man always know?"

You can still leave. It was from Correk.

Leira typed back. *I have a rep to uphold. I don't run from anything.*

Three dots appeared on her phone. *Good life plan. Stay aware. Tell her the Fixer says hello.*

Leira smiled at the text. *Subtle. See you on the flip side.*

She opened the heavy, black iron gate and let it fall shut behind her. "Seems a little on the nose, people. All that's missing is a cauldron." She walked up to a tall mahogany door and pushed the bell, listening to the first few notes of

Beethoven's Fifth Symphony. The door opened with a loud creak as Leira suppressed a crooked smile.

Ariana stood in the doorway in slim black pants and a white blouse, open at the neck. "I wasn't sure you'd come."

"You sent a very fancy invitation carried by a crow. My curiosity got the better of me."

"My uncle likes to keep the birds. He says they're like feathered dogs, only smarter and can fly. Do come in. Can I get you anything to drink?"

Leira stepped into the large foyer, looking up at the stained glass dome over her head.

"Fifteenth Century. It was brought over from Romania." Ariana gave a sly smile. "Yes, there are a lot of witches in Romania. I know you haven't known about your magic for very long, but surely you've caught on by now that a lot of fairy tales are based in truth. Follow me," said Ariana, waving a perfectly manicured hand. "I want to show you something rare, as an act of good faith. No one outside the families has ever seen it before."

Leira followed Ariana down the wide hallway to the large kitchen, passing by a cook in a stained white apron hard at work. They came to a non-descript door with an old brass handle tarnished from use. Ariana tapped it once with her wand and the door slid into the wall, the knob vanishing at the last moment. She started down the steps and looked back at Leira. "It's a very nice basement, I promise."

"Your family's history with basements isn't a pretty one." Leira went down the old stone steps, magic swirling in her feet.

"Tell me, why did you accept?" asked Ariana, still descending the stairs.

"You said this was to make an alliance. I wanted to see if you were telling the truth."

Ariana let out a snort of laughter. "Pretty iffy betting everything on whether or not I meant what I said."

"Pretty iffy turning down a chance to make peace."

Ariana stopped on the stairs and looked back at Leira. "You and I have very different ways of looking at the same thing. I wonder which one will turn out to serve its owner better." She started down again, snapping her fingers and turning on lights further down below.

"Just how far down are we going? This is starting to feel like we're going into a..." Leira touched the limestone walls, feeling a familiar buzz of energy.

"Kemana? That's because we are going into one. A private family kemana established thousands of years ago on this land. Strange, right? We were here before almost anyone else was here. It was just a muddy swamp back then, but some ancient relative liked the view of Maryland."

Leira slid her phone partly out of her pocket and saw that any signal had dropped. She kept going down the steps hearing Hagan's voice ringing in her ears. *Always take a backup with you. Little late for that.*

They finally came to the bottom of the steps, clearing the lower ceiling and entered an area as big as the town square in Hillsdale. There were even rows of shops being tended by witches and wizards. In the center was an enormous black crystal, glowing from the center and stretching up toward the cavernous ceiling.

"Does this connect to any other kemana or a train?"

"Of sorts. There's a special car that runs off the main line. It's only used by witches and wizards who have been invited here or are considered family. We set the system up a long time ago to make sure the family always has what it needs. Our kind have not always been in favor, you know," said Ariana with an edge to her voice. "Humans get uncomfortable and want to squash what's different when they're afraid. Too often they're afraid of us."

"We can change that idea this time, Ariana. Working together could go a long way toward that."

"Possibly. There has to be a reason it benefits both of us. For that to happen, you have to first have a better idea of who we really are and how we operate. All you know at the moment is a very small and jaundiced view of things. We have ruled over a vast network of witches and wizards for so long because we have worked at creating community. Do you really think we could have kept such a vast network of family in line for this long through fear? Eventually, all that results in is revolution." She smiled and gave a wink. "Sirius Pickering was a fool."

"I can't say I've underestimated your families," said Leira, looking in a shop window at silk scarves and purses. "I know the depths you'll go to when you want your way."

Ariana arched a brow, crossing her arms over her chest. "Cheeky little Elf, aren't you? You actually say what you're thinking. Gives me even more hope for a bridge of some sort."

"But I never saw that you were trying to do any kind of good." Leira's brow furrowed. "Wait, are you telling me Sirius, or his wife did things like this?"

"To a degree, they did," said Ariana, letting out a deep sigh. "Very limited. Most of this can run on its own by now. It's more accurate to say that Sirius didn't somehow kill it off. But times are changing, and the families want to know their way of life is safe. This is a part of their way of life and with the right leadership there could even be more. But it would take an end to the meaningless battles that have been sapping our resources."

"I won't argue with you on that score."

"Here's the shop I wanted to show you."

Leira looked up at the sign above the large curved front window. *First Apothecary*. "I thought the kemana was the big reveal."

"No, just a necessary reveal in order to get here."

Inside Leira could see a red Papasan chair with a sign. *Papasan Chair of Infinite Fluffiness*. "What can that chair do?"

Ariana bent down and shaded her eyes to get a better look. "The chair? It's a gimmick, really. No one knows for sure if it's naturally comfy or magically enhanced, but it's the comfiest known chair in the world. Like being hugged by an overweight friendly bear."

Leira stood up straight with a crooked smile. "Ariana, that is a very dark definition of comfy."

Ariana shrugged a shoulder and smiled, opening the door. A bell overhead tinkled. Leira walked in behind Ariana, passing by a tall vase full of bamboo sticks carved to look like little hands on the end. The little fingers started wriggling and reached out for Leira's leg. "What the fuck?" Leira looked down and read, "Witch Itch Sticks. Five dollars. I may have to get one of those." The fingers massaged her thigh, kneading the muscle. "I'm not mad at how that feels."

Along the back of the shop was a tall apothecary cabinet that stretched the entire wall. There were hundreds of black drawers with brass handles. Written on each one was the name of a plant or a mixture or a potion. "What is a Cave Lily?" asked Leira.

Ariana was busy fidgeting with a vault door, spinning a dial bigger than her hand. She stopped and glanced back over her shoulder. "They're an Oriceran plant found only in certain caves near the Mountain Gnomes and only at certain times of the year. It's the only known cure for the common cold. Mix it with different herbs and it can cure a few other things." She went back to turning the dial to the right, stopping precisely on the number thirteen.

"Why haven't you ever shared this with the world? This is your charity work. Humans would love you."

Ariana spun the dial again, stopping on the nine and pressing down on the lever getting a satisfying click and a thunk. "Two very good reasons. One, there isn't enough to go around, which would only cause friction, then resentment, and then maybe a nice battle or two. Who knows, maybe a war over a lily?" She arched a brow, looking at Leira as she pulled on the handle, leaning back to open the heavy door. "Two, humans do not always love to have answers handed to them. It's been our experience that it tends to make them suspicious and want more, right away. It's not always wise to stir the pot." She stood next to the thick, reinforced door, her hands on her hips. "This is why I brought you down here."

Leira walked closer to the door, her eyes wide with

curiosity. She glanced at the thick vault door as she went inside. "Is that for show? I mean, wouldn't wards work better?" Inside the vault, the walls on both sides were covered in deposit boxes from floor to ceiling. Each drawer had a brass plate on the front and a thin metal handle.

"There are all kinds of spells protecting this shop and this vault in particular, don't worry. Only leadership knows what's even in here." She pulled on a handle on the inside of the door, pulling it shut.

"Like the Gnomes' library on Oriceran."

"A lot like that. You know some of your background," said Ariana, sounding impressed. "We're very big on tradition if you haven't noticed. The vault has been here longer than anyone can remember." Ariana pulled out two pairs of white cotton gloves and gave one pair to Leira, putting on the others. She carefully removed a narrow drawer and set it on the tall narrow wooden table in the center. "This vault is how the apothecary got its name. It's not the first apothecary we ever built. That's in some Eastern European country somewhere. This is an apothecary of first items. Look inside."

Leira laced her gloved fingers together and peered over the edge of the drawer. Inside was a lone gold feather."

"It's a feather from the first Griffin. In that drawer," she said, pointing across the way, "is hair from the first shifter. I know, ironic, right? There was a time when we were aligned with shifters. It's what gave me the idea this time. And over in that drawer, way down there are fangs from the first Kilomea. You don't want to know how we got those." She spread her arms wide, lifting her chin. "The first of anything holds a special power that can be used when every other option has been spent and failed. This vault is our last and greatest defense. It's what helps me sleep at night."

Leira stood quietly, looking down at the shimmering gold feather. She looked around at all the boxes that stretched along the walls of the long and narrow vault. "This took a lot of trust on your part. You didn't even try to hide the location. A kemana is not an easy thing to move."

"A kemana is an impossible thing to move. We could try moving the vault if we had to, but it would put everything at risk to even attempt it."

"Thank you. You were right. Not every basement of yours is evil."

Ariana's face went blank for a moment and her hands curled into fists. But then a twitch appeared in her cheek and she rocked her head back, laughing as she pressed her gloved hands against her belly. The sound echoed off the walls as Leira waited patiently, a crooked smile on her face.

Leira let out a sigh. "I know we can at least try to work out an alliance. But before we do, I have one question I'm going to need an answer to."

"Go ahead."

"Did you set up Wolfstan Humphrey with that artifact? And if you did, are you sure you know what you're doing?"

Ariana's smile turned cold. "Wolfstan Humphrey is Sirius in Elf form. Old selfish ways that only benefit him. He will only make things worse for all of us. He needs to be contained and it was going to take something more artful to do it. Sometimes force can't be met with force."

"But will it work?"

Ariana put the box containing the Griffin feather back in its place, sliding it till it was flush with the wall. A purple wave appeared over the box for a moment, securing the ward once again. She removed her gloves as Leira did the same, giving them back. "That remains to be seen. It's always possible for someone to overcome an obstacle no one else has ever managed to do. You have proven that with the world in between. The stories about what you've done have already become legends. But, what if Wolfstan were distracted *and* brute force was applied? Would there be enough of a crack in his fortress to bring the entire thing down?" She pushed open the door to the vault and stepped outside, waiting for Leira who followed, taking one last look.

"I'm not naive enough to think the dark families have changed all their ways overnight, but I'm willing to wonder if you've changed just enough for us to work together... sometimes."

"I'll take it, Leira Berens," said Ariana, holding out her hand to shake.

"Then we have the start of a peculiar friendship."

Ariana laughed again. "Yes, it appears we do."

CHAPTER TWENTY

Leira stepped onto the underground cross town train home, jostled by a wizard getting on behind her, holding a large box. "So sorry," he said, squeezing by her to one of the last seats. Leira gave him a nod, making room for him as she grabbed onto a pole for the short ride back to N Street. She was neatly squeezed between two witches chatting about a party, and a well-dressed Dwarf in a suit with the usual bowler, but no poppy. The Dwarf had his arm hooked around a pole, reading a well-worn hardback blue book on potions. There were scribbles in all the margins with several passages underlined.

"Two ounces of bailey root," muttered Leira, absent-mindedly reading over his shoulder.

He looked up at Leira with large brown eyes, his stubby finger holding his place in the book. "Can I help you?" he said in a gravelly voice.

"Pardon me," said Leira, startled. "You have a lot of notes in your book."

The Dwarf harrumphed and put a bookmark in place,

shutting the book. "I've been healing magicals for a very long time." He took a longer look at Leira and narrowed his eyes. "Wait a minute. I know who you are. You're with the Fixer."

Leira's crooked smile appeared. "That's the first time someone has put it that way. Yes, I live with the Fixer."

The Dwarf smoothed out his snow white beard. "That makes you the Jasper Elf. I should introduce myself. My name is Dr. Barnaby Feathers, MD."

"Leira Berens, bounty hunter, I guess."

Dr Feathers nodded his head gravely. "A necessary occupation, I suppose, much like mine. Was there something that ails you?" His bushy eyebrows jiggled up and down.

"No, I'm fine. More curiosity than anything else. Lately, I keep learning about the magical world and it's been a big reminder of how little I really know. I sometimes wonder if I'll ever master it."

"The short answer is no, you won't. No one ever will, which makes this life wonderful. Hang on," he said, patting his pocket, one arm still hooked around the pole. He pulled out a card, slightly bent and smudged and handed it to Leira. "There's my number. If you ever have a question about magic, call me. Perhaps I can help. I'd like to if I can."

Leira looked down at the blank card and watched the information appear.

"That's a useful trick," he said, tapping the card in her hand. "That way if someone ever loses my card, it will look blank to a non-magical... or an enemy. My services are only available to those who wish others no harm."

"I don't wish anyone harm, but it doesn't always work out that way."

"Ah, then you qualify. Keep the card, just in case."

"Thank you," she said, tucking the card into the pocket of her jacket.

The train came to a sudden stop, blowing out a cloud of steam as the doors opened with a whoosh. A baritone voice announced, "Stand back and let riders off."

"This is my stop," said Leira. "Thank you, Dr. Feathers. I hope we meet again." She made her way between the other riders still hanging onto poles.

"Oh, it's inevitable, I'm sure."

Leira looked back at the doctor, her brow knit together. He was already buried back in his book. She stepped off quickly before the doors could close and watched as the train zipped away in another puff of steam. A red streak jettisoning down the tracks.

Leira came out of the Starbucks and turned toward home, walking down N Street. The sky was turning a deep orange as the sun began to set. She passed the side of the building and heard a loud, "Psssst. Psssst," looking around for its source. A grey rat missing a bite from one ear poked up its head from behind a large metal trash can and waved a paw at her. "Psssst."

"What a weird day," whispered Leira, looking around to see if anyone else noticed a rat waving for her to come over. "This must be what it's like for people who spot Yumfuck. I'm coming, I'm coming." She followed the rat behind the trash can and crouched out of view. "Okay, I'm here. Do you guys really talk? That would be so strange. Do squirrels talk?"

The rat rolled its eyes, its whiskers twitching. It held up a note and shook it in her face.

"Okay, I get it. Take the note. Still didn't answer my questions." Leira opened the piece of paper and read the note from the Fairhaven Willen. "This is good and bad news. How badly injured was Wolfstan?"

The rat rolled onto its back and stuck out its tongue. It popped back up again and looked up at Leira.

"Close to death. Too bad it wasn't a few inches further. Maybe this will keep him down for at least a few days. Message received. I'll take it from here."

The rat gave a nod and took off, running in front of a woman taking a shortcut from the alley. She let out a yelp and threw an empty cup at the rat who neatly dodged it. "Rats! Don't you hate them?" asked the woman as she passed Leira.

"Not anymore," muttered Leira, pocketing the note and turning back toward home.

"There you are!" Angel came tripping down her steps in pale blue pedal pushers and espadrilles, a glass of red wine in her hand. Her front door was wide open behind her. "Nicole and Norah stopped by after work and I was hoping to catch you. Come on in and say hello," she said, flinging an arm around Leira. "Even if it's just a few minutes. It's been a long week already. It's almost the end of the month and I had to reconcile all the accounts today. My eyes are practically crossed. How was your day? You look like you're glowing." Angel's eyes widened and her face reddened as she looked up toward her house, but no one was at the windows. "I'm so sorry." She lifted a hand by her mouth and whispered. "I would never tell anyone. I mean, I didn't mean glowing, glowing. You know, like... magicky glowing." She waggled her fingers in the air making Leira laugh.

"Oh good, you're laughing. Whew," said Angel.

"You reminded me of an old friend. Sure, why not. Let me text Correk and let him know where I am." Leira looked down at her phone and saw the three texts from Angel. "Oh, I missed your messages. Sorry about that. I was in an area with poor reception."

"No worries. I kept an eye out for you," said Angel as they went up the stairs to her house. "Sometimes you just want to have your girlfriends around you to make the day better. You know what I mean?"

Leira waited for Angel to plunge ahead in the conversation without her, still smiling. They got to the door and she quickly typed a message to Correk. *Interesting day. This time in a good way. Lots to tell you. Met a doctor on the train. But next door with the friends. Be home soon.*

"Nicole got the thumbs up on a big deal today so she's ready to celebrate. A mixed-use beauty in Fairfax. That's what started the whole thing. She showed up on my doorstep with a tasty bottle of wine."

Angel plunged inside, disappearing toward the kitchen. Leira's phone pinged and she pulled it back out. *You made it to the other side. I'll keep dinner warm. Did you know YTT has a new friend?*

Dad still there? Leira quickly typed, stopping in her tracks and wondering if she should head home.

Left a while ago but YTT is having a sleepover. He let Nibbler in his room. It was followed by a surprised emoji face.

"Leira, you coming? Red or white?"

Leira smiled and put her phone away, heading into the kitchen. "Glass of red," she called out. She came into the wide open space and saw Norah and Nicole sitting at the island. "Leira!" they cheered, holding up their glasses, beaming.

I like this. Girlfriends. Who knew? She stood there for a moment taking it in, blinking hard and smiling till her dimples were showing. *It's like Mitzi and Craig and even Toni and Jack were training me for this.*

Angel waved her hands up and down. "Woohoo, Leira. You leave us for a sec?"

"What kind of day did you have?" Norah sipped her wine, standing up to lean over the island and snag a square of pepper cheese.

"I was getting to know different parts of the city. Job related, can't say much."

"That is one thing about our town," said Nicole. "It's a company town and the real business is secrets of all kinds."

"Here, here," said Angel, raising her glass.

"Thank goodness we have each other to stay grounded," said Norah. "What's that old saying? We're only as sick as our secrets. Everybody needs someone that they can tell the absolute truth."

"Well, I don't know about you three, but you can count on me to listen," said Angel, refilling her glass, "and to keep it stored away to the grave. Mostly because I forget, but also because you are my squad."

"To the squad!" Nicole held up her glass and the others joined in, including Leira, who cleared her throat.

"Then I have kind of a secret to tell all of you." She avoided looking at Angel whose eyes had grown wider. "I... I have never had a squad of girlfriends before. I had an interesting childhood..."

"Heard that."

"There's a lot of that going around."

Leira sat down at the island next to Norah, "and I never got around to the whole best friend thing, much less an entire squad. You guys are my first." She grinned sheepishly as Angel let out a relieved sigh. Norah put her arm around her, tilting her head. "I am honored, Leira Berens and you were just waiting for the right squad. Shows good taste."

Leira lifted her glass again. "To the friends' squad."

"To the ride or die friends' squad," said Nicole. "Little wordy. We can work on that. Okay, okay," she said, brushing her hair out of her face. "Come what may, we have each other's back."

"If it's the last good thing we do," added Leira, as everyone cheered.

CHAPTER TWENTY-ONE

Yumfuck Tiberius Troll waited under the green wooden bench with Nibbler by his side, waiting for Samuel Akins. The small park was mostly empty except for people using it to cut through on their way to lunch or back to work. Nibbler lay on his back, rolling from side to side in the soft grass, trilling.

"You're easy to have around, Nibbler. You don't say much, and you eat very little. We are going to get along great."

Nibbler sat up on his elbows, the wind rustling his purple hair. "I won't be here very long. I have to be back to Oriceran by tomorrow. My mother is stopping by the cabin with a few hundred of my siblings."

Yumfuck leaned out from the bench, looking for Samuel in the distance but there was no sign of him. "You know it's okay to talk around other magicals. Most are good people."

Nibbler pulled his furry knees up to his chin. "It was magicals that ripped away my former person. I'm good."

"Yeah, the people who did it were some real mother-fuckers," said Yumfuck, shaking his head.

"Motherfuckers!" said Nibbler, shaking his tiny paw in the air.

"Bad guys like that are taking the fun right out of that word," tsked Yumfuck, leaning out again to take another look. At the edge of the park behind two women in yoga pants carrying mats was Samuel, shuffling along and tapping his cane. "Something's not right," muttered Yumfuck, scampering up the cement side of the bench to the tallest point to get a better look.

A young man in a *Go Bison* sweatshirt did a double take and pulled out a small notebook, jotting down an idea. "Stories just write themselves."

"I know what you mean, dude," said the troll. "Rock on." Yumfuck held up his paw, waggling it from side to side.

The young man swallowed hard, looking around for confirmation from someone else. "Little furry dude is talking to me. I knew it! I knew aliens were real."

"No pictures," said Yumfuck holding up his paws, still trying to get a better view of Samuel. "I gave my word."

The two women got closer and one elbowed the other, nodding at the troll perched on top of the bench. The other woman looked over and took in the young man leaning over to chat with Yumfuck, her mouth opening into a perfect 'O'. "That's not good," she said, sliding a wand out of the middle of her rolled up mat. "Never was, never will be," she said, pointing her wand at the young man. He froze, his face in a wide grin.

Yumfuck looked down at Nibbler and put a claw to his

lips. He looked back up at the two witches and held very still.

The taller witch came over to Yumfuck as she slid her wand back into the middle of her mat. She leaned close to his small face and arched a brow. Nibbler hid below holding his breath. "You know better than that, troll. Just a warning this time, but you need to stay out of sight."

"You're lucky we're late for our class. Go on, get below." The other witch adjusted her mat and looked at her watch. "Do we move him at all?"

"Maybe a little," said the witch, straightening the young man and pointing him in another direction. 'That ought to do it. Now you..." She turned to say something else to Yumfuck, but he had already climbed nimbly down to the ground and was safely behind the bench, holding onto Nibbler's trembling paw.

"Hmph, that was easy. I wish all our assignments were like that." The two witches took one last look around and went back to trying to decide where to go for margaritas after class.

Samuel was not far behind them and took a seat on the bench, groaning as he sat down. He ignored the man standing still and waited patiently till he started to move again, wondering why he had stopped walking. It didn't take long before the young man was on his way again, ambling down the walk, scratching his head.

"You can come out now," said Samuel, rolling his cane between his hands. "Check first to be sure, but I don't hear a thing."

Yumfuck looked around and pulled Nibbler behind

him, standing behind a tall dandelion by Samuel's shoe. "That was close."

"Too close," squeaked Nibbler.

"You brought back your friend! I'm honored," said Samuel. "What was that about? It sounded like you were on the verge of being arrested. I was ready to come in swinging."

"Remember that gang of magicals that helped you out a long time ago? That was two of their agents. I got a little sloppy waiting for you."

"I'll say," chimed in Nibbler, earning a side eye from Yumfuck.

Samuel chuckled as he slumped back against the bench, wincing as his shoulder made contact. "Long day. Glad it's almost over."

Yumfuck scurried up Samuel's pant leg, still pulling a reluctant Nibbler behind him.

"You're hurt. What happened to you?" Yumfuck stopped at Samuel's elbow, looking up at his friend's face. There was a green patch partially hidden by the sunglasses he was normally wearing, quickly turning darker colors. Yumfuck jumped down to Samuel's lap where he had left Nibbler and reached out for Samuel's hand, holding it gently between his paws. "You're my friend, Samuel. Let us help you."

Nibbler nodded his head vigorously.

"Oh, for Pete's sake. Fine, Nibbler is nodding that he's in too. I am Batfuck," said the troll, standing up straighter with his paws on his hips.

Nibbler stood up and did the same. "Yeah!"

"Sounds like you have a sidekick," said Samuel, wearily.

"I got myself a Robin," said Yumfuck, beaming. "But you have to trust us enough to tell us what happened. Did the government find you?"

"No, no, nothing like that." Samuel shook his head, wiping his face with his hand. Nibbler gasped and pointed at the burn marks on the back of Samuel's hand.

Yumfuck felt a ribbon of anger course through his little body but he pressed his paws together, taking in a deep breath and holding it, before letting it go. "Anger clouds judgment," he whispered to Nibbler. "First lesson in being a successful crime fighter. Remain calm." He took back Samuel's hand. "Start from the beginning."

"Maybe you're right. This is too big for me to handle on my own. I know firsthand what you little fellas can do." Samuel's shoulders sagged but he lifted his chin. "There's a group of young thugs who have been hanging around my building. Maybe five or six of them. They've been hassling me and a few others, trying to get us to pay them protection money. I'll be damned if I pay somebody just to be able to walk the streets in peace."

"This job is gonna be over in time to get ice cream," said Yumfuck.

"Yum... ice cream," said Nibbler.

"There's hope for you yet, kid," said Yumfuck.

"There's a wrinkle. A kind of big wrinkle." Samuel shifted on the bench trying to lift his injured shoulder. "Back when I lost my sight..." He pressed his lips together, swallowing hard. "Well, there's a few things that have stuck with me. One of them is the smell of a magic fireball. There's nothing quite like it. It has an acrid scent to it that's not like anything else. I've smelled it on these teen thugs more than once. It's the reason I haven't done anything more. I think someone could get really hurt. Maybe I could tell those Silver Griffins about them."

"Not a bad plan," said Yumfuck, "but they'll want to go by the book. If there's no proof, there will just be a warning."

Samuel held up his hands, shaking his head. "That could make things even worse."

"I have a different idea. I think there's a way to bring along some seasoned crime fighters who would be willing to bend the rules and get justice done. Let's go find these hooligans giving magic a bad name."

"The worst!" yelled Nibbler, leaping into the air.

"You're really starting to come out of your shell," said Yumfuck, just as Nibbler lost his footing and slid down the side of Samuel's leg, rolling across the bench.

"Okay, well, we'll work on that," said Yumfuck, putting out his hand to help pull him back up. "First, though we need to make one or two stops. I need to talk to a few friends and pick up a few supplies."

CHAPTER TWENTY-TWO

"Okay, you know what to do?" Yumfuck hid in one pocket of Samuel's jacket and Nibbler was in the other. They were standing down the block from his apartment building, about to cross the street.

"I think I have it. You really think this will work?"

Yumfuck poked out his head. "If we were by ourselves, I'd still say we have a pretty good shot. But with our friends, I know we're unbeatable." Yumfuck put his paw into mouth and let out a loud, high-pitched whistle.

The doors of a restored white Cadillac Calais opened up and out stepped Portia and George. "Come on, that was the signal. It's time to rumble," said Portia. The back doors opened, and Elijah slid out with Marcy and Emmett not far behind. "I have not been this jazzed up since the nineteen sixties and we took down that gang of wizards muscling our neighborhood on the Grand Concourse in the Bronx," said Emmett. "There's a nice mix of magic and adrenaline running through these old veins. Let me at em."

"Remember the plan," said Marcy in a calming voice.

"We need to use some finesse, so we don't bring the Silver Griffins or the Feds down on our heads."

"I got it. We break up in groups and keep it moving. We want to scare and maybe wound," said Emmett, rubbing his hands together.

"Emmett..." said Marcy, arching an eyebrow.

"It may be necessary," said George. "These things happen on missions."

"They sure sound ready to go," said Samuel. Yumfuck could feel his heart beating faster. "They like to help when they can. It's kind of been their path their entire lives." He looked over at the other pocket that was shaking. Nibbler had raised his head to look out, his eyes wide. Yumfuck gave him the thumbs up and braced himself. "Ready when you are."

"Well, it's now or never." Samuel put out his cane as the older magicals dropped back, forming a lopsided V behind him, marching down the sidewalk. Just as they had been instructed by Yumfuck, they slowed their walk, with Elijah even trying out a shuffle. George walked stooped over with Portia's hand in the crook of his arm. They neared the building and could see three teenagers sitting on the front steps.

A lanky Light Elf with a buzz cut on the sides and floppy blonde curls on the top of his head stood up, his baggy shorts hanging down past his knees. "Hey Pops, glad to see you made it home safely. You thought anymore about our little conversation?" The Light Elf bounced his fingers in the air, a small fireball on the end of each one.

"Not now, Ralph." Samuel instinctively ducked his head

down. Emmett kept watching the wiry tall kid in front of Samuel and the other two still on the steps.

Behind Samuel, Portia and George veered to the left, walking closer to the curb and closing the gap between themselves and the building. Portia slyly slid out two wands, passing one to George Elijah stayed right behind Samuel as Marcy and Emmett hugged the building.

"Oh, they're not with you," said Ralph, the fireballs still dancing on his fingertips. "Too bad. Looks like you're all alone again." He glanced back at his friends to give a wink just as Yumfuck leaned out of his pocket with a tiny sling-shot and a piece of gravel. He shot at one of the fireballs, putting it out and sunk back in the pocket. Ralph felt the fire extinguish and jerked his head back, confused. "What the fuck?" He curled up a lip, exposing a missing tooth. "That's never happened before." He blew on the finger, creating another fireball, slowly getting back his bravado. "We're gonna need that money we talked about, sooner rather than later. Now Jamie..." He looked back at the Light Elf sitting on the steps who raised his hand in a cocky salute.

Yumfuck leaned out of the pocket again with two pieces of gravel, neatly shooting them to take out two of the fire-balls on Ralph's fingers. Ralph spun back around and looked at his hand, his brow furrowed. Sweat was already forming on his high forehead. "What the... How are you doing that old man? You're not a magical."

"No, but we are," said Elijah. "Duck!" Samuel did as they had practiced and ducked down, giving Elijah a clear view to pitch a volley of small fireballs at Ralph, burning holes in a tic tac toe pattern up and down his t-shirt. Ralph spun his arms around wildly at his side, regaining his composure enough to pat his chest. Two of his fingers, however, reignited a couple of the fires causing him to blow on his hand and pat his chest at the same time.

Jamie and the other Light Elf hopped off the steps, ready to join in the fight but Portia and George already had out their wands. "I'm really gonna enjoy this more than I should," said Portia. "Parietem affixit!" She swirled her wand in a circle at the two Light Elves and watched with delight as they flew backward, slamming into the brick wall of the building and sticking. They hung in place with their feet dangling, waving their arms and doing their best to pull in magic and get themselves down.

Ralph looked back and forth rapidly between his friends and the magicals surrounding him. "Kenny! Ricky! Get out here!" Two more Light Elves came barreling out the front door of the building where they had been lurking, tripping down the steps. The round, dark haired Elf's mouth dropped open at the sight of his friends pinned to the building and almost ran into the back of the other Light Elf. "Kenny, what the hell are you doing?" Ricky put out his elbow jabbing him in his belly, but he was also quick enough to swoop his arm around, pushing out an energy pulse. Marcy and Emmett were ready for him, countering it with a wave of their own that shoved back hard enough to make his teeth clack.

"What is happening?" yelled Ralph, enraged as he reached out with both hands to try and throttle Samuel around his neck.

"Now!" yelled Yumfuck and Nibbler, to his credit, immediately jumped out of his pocket, along with

Yumfuck. They were growing before they hit the ground into giant, furry pandas with green and purple hair on the top of their heads. Ralph leaned back in horror, his hands still outstretched, hanging in mid-air.

Nibbler swiped at him, tearing what was left of his burned t-shirt off his body leaving a red claw mark down the front of his pale chest. Yumfuck stood up on his hind legs and roared, falling to all four paws and pounding his way toward Kenny and Ricky. Kenny panicked and shoved Ricky in front, turned and ran. Marcy threw a fireball in his direction, lighting up the back of his pants and burning a hole clear through to his white underpants.

"Are we winning?" asked Samuel who was still sticking to the plan and was staying perfectly still, clutching his cane close to his body.

"We are kicking ass!" growled Nibbler, beating his paws against his chest.

Yumfuck picked up Ricky over his head and tossed him like a bean bag into the street near Portia and George. "My turn!" yelled George, spinning his wand in tight circles, which spun Ricky in the air like a top. It wasn't long before the remaining miscreants were laying on the pavement, spent and a little charred in places.

"Do you mind?" asked Elijah, his irises moving in different directions to make sure no one was thinking of restarting the fight.

"Be my guest," said Samuel. "Wow. That sounded like one hell of a battle."

"If you ever return to this block..." said Elijah.

Portia bent over Ralph and said, "If you ever go near our friend, Samuel or anyone in this building..."

Marcy came over and nudged him with her shoe. "If we ever find out you were scamming anyone, human or magical..."

George came and stood by Portia. "We will hunt you down."

Emmett joined them. "And we have the time and the skill to do it. Probably only take an afternoon and we'll finish the job."

"Now get out of here and never come back!" yelled Samuel, getting a cheer from everyone else.

Ralph rolled over on his knees and slowly stood up, taking his time as Jamie and his compatriot slid off the wall and Ricky picked himself out of the street. Yumfuck and Nibbler gave one last roar together, speeding them up as they took off running in the same direction anyone last saw Kenny.

"Good riddance," yelled Samuel, shaking his cane. "That felt good," he said, as Yumfuck and Nibbler shrunk back down to size and came and stood in front of him.

"You have a lot of new friends, Samuel."

"That's right," said Portia, taking George's hand.

"Never forget, we operate better together than all by ourselves," said Yumfuck.

"We are a team," shouted Nibbler, catching himself by surprise. "I'm part of a team," he whispered. Yumfuck hugged his friend, squeezing tight. "You're gonna be alright, Nibbler. Whew, you're gonna be just fine."

Yumfuck pushed another chair over by his desk. "That one's for you," he said to Nibbler, growing to three feet tall. He waited for Nibbler to grow and settle himself into the chair and then he climbed up on the rungs, getting on his knees to pull out the letter to Hagan that he had started and his favorite Green Lantern pen with green ink.

Update: Boy, was I right. So much has happened since I started this letter! Hey, my new friend found a name. It's Nibbler and he's spending the night. He's right here with me. I'll get him to leave a paw print when I'm done. You'll never believe the day we had. We teamed up with the magicals down the street and Nibbler and me chased off a bunch of teenage thugs. They were messing with my other friend, Samuel. Best part is, Nibbler found his courage. It was amazing. I have to go. Correk is going to help us make s'mores over the kitchen stove and tell us a couple of old Oriceran stories. Write me back soon.

Your Friend for Life,
Yumfuck Tiberius Troll

CHAPTER TWENTY-THREE

There was an anguished lowing coming from the workroom. The plants outside on the sanctuary grounds bent toward the mournful sound. The Gardener of the Dark Forest sat astride the lion, shaking his large head, rubbing his antlers against the bark of a large oak tree. Behind him, a small herd of iridescent deer grazed in the clearing, chewing new leaves off the lower branches of the trees. They glowed with a soft, white glimmer that backlit the Gardener. The vines in his hair wove in and out, the blossoms opening toward the light.

Hagan and Rose came walking down a path that wove between the buildings and saw the Gardener patiently watching the workroom building. "What do you suppose that's about?" asked Rose, holding Hagan's hand.

Hagan let out a sigh and adjusted his pants with his other hand. "Harkin and that young witch from Austin are..." He struggled for the right words. "They're going to attempt to really fix a wrong."

Rose looked at the Gardener's somber expression. "Maybe we should leave them all to it."

"You always do know the best course of action. I have a letter to write anyway," said Hagan as they turned back in the direction of their cottage.

Inside the workroom a large black Aberdeen Angus bull stomped its front hooves, too exhausted to protest much further. Joints had been replaced with gears and other machine parts. In the center entire organs were now electronics bolstering the animal's abilities but not without a painful consequence.

Lily Sharpton laid her head gently on the bull's back, shutting her eyes as a tear rolled down her cheek. The soft dark fur rubbed against her cheek as the bull snorted and shifted again, trying to get comfortable. But it was not going to be impossible. "I'm going to try and help," she whispered. "I'm so sorry this was done to you." She ran her hand up and down the cow's back, careful to avoid the edge where it dropped off into machinery and electronics. "He will pay for everything he's done," she said, not wanting to evoke Wolfstan Humphrey's name.

"Today, we start with this beast," said Harkin standing just behind her with a syringe filled with forty grams of chloral hydrate. "Correk has taught me that lesson. Do what you can where you are. Don't discount how valuable that is to someone."

"Will that be enough?"

"It'll be enough to lightly sedate him and give us enough time to get him onto the stretcher. If we fail, what we're doing will end his misery, which is valuable for this creature. Nothing with a beating heart should be tortured like this. If we succeed, then we may just bring hope to a lot of magicals who have been butchered. Correk told me about the army Wolfstan is building. I wish I had killed him in Trevilsom when I had the chance. It would have been worth it."

Lily covered her face with her hands, pressing her fingers against her temples. She dropped her hands and shook them out. "Enough of my hand wringing. There's work to be done." She pushed her hair behind her ears and lifted her chin. "Let's get started."

"You've been really brave, you know. Invaluable, really, and you risked everything."

Lily's face warmed as the animal lowed again, gently shaking his head. "In the scheme of things, I risked a job and I got away without a scratch. Well, maybe a small scar," she said, glancing at her wrist. "I was just following my aunt's example, you know. Aunt Lois has been on more missions and faced more monsters."

The bull stomped his foot making his body shake and cried out in pain, startling Lily. "Enough. Do it," she said, determined.

"Get ready. I can use a spell to help maneuver him into place, but he weighs over eighteen hundred pounds. If he falls on you before the spell takes affect it could do some damage."

Lily bit her lip, her hands still on the beast as Harkin injected him. "Is the Gardener ever going to come inside?"

"No, he's keeping vigil outside. We only have about ten minutes at best till he's out," said Harkin. "And only an hour till he will start to wake up."

The young witch looked at Harkin, pressing her lips together, holding back what she wanted to say.

"I know... *if* he wakes up." Harkin pulled gently on the halter till the Angus was lined up with the platform he had made especially for the large bull. Harkin pulled in energy, letting it rise through his body till his eyes glowed. "Morbi ut papilio. Quasi folium componere. Fugit velut puer."

The Aberdeen Angus opened his mouth and snuffled the air, his tongue lazily licking his lip. His eyes slowly shut and opened again as his body began to rise and turn in the air. Harkin moved his arms, deliberate in his directions for the slow operation. Once the bull was on his side, Harkin swept his hands to the right and the animal came down to rest on the structure. He let out a rush of air, his lips lifting to reveal his large teeth as his eyes finally shut. "Step one, done and successful. Help me move the hood in place."

"I wish we still had the bowl." Lily lifted her side of the delicate curved dome, settling it into place. It rested over the body of the bull with the head exposed.

"The shifters needed it more right now. We need to figure out how to solve this without the use of one small artifact, or we are in dire straits. I've made all the necessary adjustments based on what happened with Peyton and your research. I have an ounce of optimism, even." He put his hand on the bull's leg, letting his energy surround the Angus, checking the animal's status. "Okay, he's completely out. We're ready for step two."

Lily and Harkin stood beside the machine, neither one ready to push any buttons, turn any dials, utter any spells. "My stomach is in knots." Lily sucked in air, holding it for a moment. "I mean, I don't want to make it worse. This isn't like the experiments I'm used to running. I'm used to individual cells. This is an entire organism that can feel joy and pain."

"You've already proven that the cells can mutate with the use of magic. Now we need to find out how far that will go." He checked the settings one more time and before he could think about it any longer, turned the dial. The machinery gave off a low hum as a neon blue line of light zipped across the surface from one side to the other. It was quickly followed by another glowing stripe three inches away, and then another and another. Once the entire space was covered, the stripes started from the other direction rapidly creating a luminous blue grid. The hum gave way to a sizzle and pop as Lily's mouth opened ever so slightly, and she held her breath.

"I think it might be fucking working." said Harkin in a hushed voice. The magic continued to mix with the engineered parts, radiating off the machine, shoving out into the room. Harkin gritted his teeth and put out an arm, pushing Lily further away as he took a step back. He glanced back at the entrance to Peyton's old room, the pressure building against his chest.

At last the machine decelerated and the blue lines reversed themselves, removing the pattern. Lily reached out and grasped Harkin's hand giving it a quick squeeze before she let go. The sizzle reduced to a hum and eventually to a stillness that filled the room. The bull continued to sleep peacefully, occasionally fluttering its long lashes.

"You look," said Lily, still standing a few feet from the machine. "I'm sorry, I can't bring myself to do it," she said, shaking her head.

Harkin's brow furrowed and he took each step slowly, finally getting close enough to look under the dome. He let out a short gasp, tears filling his eyes. The experiment had worked but had only gone so far. The bull's torso was rebuilt halfway, stopping abruptly behind the middle of the ribs. The liver had been reconfigured, but the descending colon was still plastic tubing. Harkin rubbed his chin, blinking his eyes. He placed a hand on the bull's head, pressing down with his hand. He swallowed hard and knit his brows together. "Cinis cinerem. Reditur contra velum," he whispered, tears dripping onto the cow's head. "Rest in peace at last." The animal's breathing became labored and halting until at last it finally stopped. The gears stopped turning and the barely audible whir from the electronics that remained disappeared.

Lily's eyes were wide and shining and her hands were in fists at her side. "I haven't done nearly enough," she said, haltingly. "Until he's punished, I'm not finished."

Harkin stood up and lifted his shirt to wipe his face, putting it back in place. "It almost worked. It was almost enough."

"There are so many times in life where *almost* is closer to nothing than to having something. This is one of those times."

"You're wrong, Lily. You know better than anyone that science can be a cruel bitch when it comes to progress. It's made in small failures mixed with bits and pieces of success."

"I know you're right, but there's so much at stake and when we fail..."

"When we fail, someone may die. I have lived with that

thought for a very long time. But we're not going to stop at this juncture. We're going to move forward and keep going till Wolfstan is defeated. Even if it's not us, there are others who would take our place. He will not win."

Lily moved closer and ran her hand along the bull's head. "What's the next step?"

"We have to get that ring back. I believe it holds the key. It's time to take the risk and bring it home, even if it means bringing Wolfstan Humphrey closer to us."

"It's time we face him head on anyway."

Harkin nodded and walked toward the screen door, pushing it open and stepping outside. The lion lifted its head and looked at Harkin, letting out a low growl. Harkin shook his head solemnly and saw the flash of anger pass across the Gardener's face. The Gardener pressed gently against the lion's ribs as the large cat turned and they padded deeper into the sanctuary.

Lily came outside and stood next to Harkin, letting the gentle Texas breeze cool her off. "How'd he take it, do you think?"

"Poorly, as he should. A war is coming, not just a battle and it will be for the fate of how we all live once the gates are opened. There can be no reasoned truce this time. We will have to win it all or lose far too much. We need that damn ring."

CHAPTER TWENTY-FOUR

L eira drove the Mustang up Route Six-Six-Two in Leesburg, Virginia, turning onto Lucketts Road. She glanced over at Correk shaking the empty Starburst bag upside down. His lap was filled with colorful little pieces of waxed paper, some of them drifting onto the floorboards. Correk harrumphed and brushed the papers off his lap.

"You're picking those up later." Leira pointed over the steering wheel at the wide open sky. "Will you look at that sunset? What if we waited to go down in the kemana till the sun goes down? It's so beautiful out here away from the city."

"We'll lose our reservation. Plus, we can't be late to meet the Willen for the hand off." Correk slurped the last of a Dr. Pepper in a tall, slim bottle and put it back in the cup holder. "There, happy? Very neat."

"One small step for magical kind... Restaurants in the kemana take reservations? There are that many magicals in this area that want to have dinner underground. Really?"

Correk picked up the plastic bag and shook it one more

time. "Magicals come from all over to eat at this place. It has three Rafkin stars."

"Nothing more is coming out of that bag. I can see that from here." Leira stopped at the red light and waited even though there were no other cars on the road. "Is a Rafkin star a big deal?"

Correk looked taken aback. "Even I know what a Rafkin star means. A panel of magicals rate all the finer kemana restaurants. Even getting one star is amazing. Aha!" He pulled a pink Starburst from between the seats and held it up, triumphant.

"Did you not eat lunch? We've only been driving for a little over an hour." She pulled the Mustang up in front of the oddly shaped green clapboard store. Over the far left side of the porch was a sign reading, *Luckett's General Store*. On the far right of the long extension to the porch were doors painted in red and white unattached from all sides except the bottom with large gaps everywhere else. Stuffed behind them were odds and ends for sale. At the end of the porch was another sign that read, *Broken Barn Arena*.

"We left DC's borders. It's officially a road trip."

"That happened about fifteen minutes after we got in the car." Leira parked the car and stopped the engine, opening her door. She got out and smoothed down the front of her little black dress. Her large gold hoop earrings dangled, hitting her neck. "How are you going to make it home? You ate everything you had on the way here."

"General store," said Correk, tapping the side of his head. "Always thinking."

Leira snorted with laughter, giving a crooked grin. "Always thinking of something. You're in a good mood."

"All those snacks I had? They were from my stash. The furry menace has not been able to find the new hiding place."

Leira walked around the car and wrapped her arms around Correk, tilting her head back to kiss him. "I've seen you less excited over successful Fixer missions."

"This one is personal," he said, finally laughing. "Okay, maybe I can skip it this time. We need to get in the kemana anyway. If you're more than five minutes late, your table is gone." He led Leira around to the back of the store past an oversized wooden birdhouse that was in the shape of a country church with a green roof. Next to it were different stacks of wooden chairs in different styles, leaning against each other. Buried in the middle was an old storm shelter dug into the ground a few feet from the building. Two wooden doors with chipped white paint covered over the entrance. A large padlock rusted with age was looped through two thick metal rings, keeping it closed. Correk went to the side of the shelter and brushed off a stone covered in leaves, whispering, "Open sesame."

"Really? That's a spell too?" said Leira, excited.

Correk grinned, resting on one knee. "No, I did that one just for you." Carved into the rock were three symbols. A triangle, a square and an infinity symbol. Correk pulled in just enough energy and pushed on the infinity symbol, releasing the padlock.

"How do you keep humans from pushing the buttons?"

"They push them all the time, especially children but nothing happens. It takes a little magic to open this kemana. However, if a magical pushes the wrong button... Well, it's the same as Hillsdale."

"Good to know." Leira unhooked the lock and the door lifted under its own powers revealing stone steps that wound down into darkness.

"Bounty hunters first," said Correk, smiling. Leira stepped onto the stairs and started down, trusting that another step would be there as the darkness grew thicker around her and the light from above got further away. Correk stepped inside and started down the stairs, waving his hand over his head. The door automatically closed, the lock finding its place and clicking shut.

For a moment the passageway was inky black but just as suddenly crystals embedded in the walls every few feet began to glow with a warm, rosy light. Leira kept going down the stairs, descending further into the ground, adjusting the thin leather strap of her black velvet purse on her shoulder. "I would have worn flats if I'd thought about what it takes to get into a kemana," said Leira.

"Easily rectified," said Correk, coming up behind her and easily lifting Leira into his arms, surprising her and making her laugh.

"Now this is how you make an entrance," she said, putting an arm around his neck and resting against his muscled chest. "Travel snacks really look good on you."

"I thought you'd never notice."

"Oh, I notice. On a regular basis, I notice."

Correk kissed her forehead in response and went down the remaining steps and around the last curve, stepping into a bustling street. A sandwich board near the entrance read, Welcome to Mayfield in bright blue letters that kept changing shape. *Streetlights Go Out at Eleven PM, Sharp*, it read next. *Mivree Smoothies Two for One at Charley's,* followed by *Pickpockets Will Be Prosecuted*, and ended with, *Enjoy Your Stay!*

To the right of the street was a gleaming silver crystal that pulsed with light. Shops were arranged in a half moon in front of it, separated by a small park and a street. Correk started walking toward the shops still carrying Leira in his arms, a contented smile on his face.

Leira started to say something but changed her mind, crossing her ankles. "Good evening," she said to an older couple passing them on the sidewalk. The witch smiled and nodded to Leira as her husband playfully elbowed her. "That used to be us," he said. "Maybe we can try that again," which got a giggle from the witch and a wink.

"I could get used to this," said Leira. "I'm surprised this hasn't happened sooner."

Correk kissed her on the forehead again. "You are a different person these days. I'm gonna risk it and say you've become more easygoing. If I'd tried this not too long ago you would have protested and then picked me up just to even things out."

"Can't say you're wrong. I wonder what else I've missed out on. Hello." Leira waved to a Light Elf maneuvering down the sidewalk carrying two large bags of groceries. The Elf harrumphed as he squeezed past, dropping an apple that rolled along the ground. "Sorry," called Leira as they kept going, passing a barber shop with wizards and Elves sitting in chairs by the window. A wizard took off his hat and waved with it, smiling broadly.

"We should do this all the time," said Leira. "Like make it a thing."

"Okay, we're here," said Correk, gently putting Leira

down. He smoothed out the front of his shirt and put out his hand for her. "Right on time."

"Genleigh's," said Leira, reading the name of the restaurant. Correk opened the door and let Leira walk in ahead of him. They went up to the tall stand with a gold G on the front of it and waited for the witch with piles of blonde curly hair to look up at them.

"Reservation for Correk and Leira," Correk said. "Seven thirty."

"Oh, right, of course!" The hostess snapped her fingers in the air. "Linus!" A thin, bony wizard in black pants and a white shirt with a black bow tie came swiftly to her side. "Tell Vernon, the Fixer is here."

Linus startled and looked at Correk, his mouth opening and shutting. "Linus!" snapped the hostess. "Pull it together and go tell Vernon. "Linus's body shook down to his toes, but he started moving, weaving his way between the tables covered in white linen and diners all craning their necks to get a look.

"Wow, looks like we could have gotten a reservation on any day," said Leira, grinning. "You're a fucking celebrity!"

An older witch sitting at a nearby table wearing a large crystal pin on an ample bust tsked at Leira, frowning.

"It's fucking okay," said Correk to the witch. "She's fucking with me." The woman harrumphed and twisted back around in her seat. "You keep doing you," said Correk, squeezing Leira's hand.

"My hero." Leira reached up and kissed Correk, lingering with her lips against his.

"Uh... ahem..."

Leira pulled back to see the hostess standing there

along with a tall Light Elf with a long brown braid down his back, wearing a white apron, tied at the waist.

"You must be Vernon," said Correk. "We have a reservation?"

"Of course you do! Right this way." Vernon held out his arm and started walking, making his way between the tables. "I'm so sorry we kept you waiting. It's been a while since a Fixer has graced our humble restaurant. Please do give Turner Underwood our regards." Violins floated through the air with bows playing back and forth across the strings.

Vernon stopped at a small curved banquette on the far wall in the middle of the room. "Madame?"

Leira let go of Correk's hand and slid onto the banquette, putting her purse next to her. The candles on the table flickered and a flame appeared. A red rose grew up out of the milky white glass vase.

Correk pulled out the wooden chair and sat down opposite her as Vernon handed them small, handwritten menus. "May I recommend the trout tonight. It is fresh, caught today and served to perfection with an orange saffron sauce with wild rice. Can I start you with wine?"

Correk looked at Leira and tilted his head. "Trust me?"

"Always."

He took the menu from Leira and handed them both back to Vernon. "Why don't you surprise us, and yes, we'd love some wine."

Vernon clapped his hands together in delight. "What a splendid idea!" He rushed off to the kitchen with Linus in tow, giving orders in a low voice.

"That was a genius idea," said Leira. "Is this what life is

going to be like whenever we go around magicals? No wonder Turner Underwood has so many baby mommas."

"You're my one and only, forever."

"You know, Mom keeps bringing up the idea of us having kids. We've never talked about anything like that. I don't even know if you want kids. I'm pretty sure you like them."

Correk spit out a little of his water, coughing. He covered his mouth with his fist and swallowed, reaching out to take another sip of water as an amused Leira watched him. "Of course I like kids," he said at last. Leira furrowed her brow waiting for more. "Yes, yes, I think I want kids," he sputtered.

"Think? When are you ever not sure about what you want?"

"You caught me off guard." He took in a deep breath and let it out slowly. "Okay, yes, I think about it a lot since I met you. I definitely want children with you. Maybe not... today?"

"Okay, calm down, I'm not pregnant. It's not today. I was just curious. Okay, second hot topic. What are your thoughts on bringing the ring back within our circle? Somehow Wolfstan will hear about it. He always does."

"I think it's necessary," said Correk, wiping his mouth on a white cloth napkin with an embroidered gold G on it. "This is when Harkin needs it and if Wolfstan is really badly injured..."

"We can only hope."

"Then this is the best time to retrieve it. He's distracted."

"Smart of you to combine it with date night as our cover."

"It's not really our cover. I've been wanting to try this restaurant for a long time."

"Ever since you heard about its third Rafkin star."

"Exactly."

Vernon came back with a long, narrow ceramic plate full of shucked oysters. "A little something to get you started and keep the mood going," said Vernon, with a wink. "These were some of Turner's favorite kind. I hope it suits the two of you as well."

Vernon quickly disappeared back into the kitchen as Leira put her hand on the table and Correk took it, intertwining his fingers with hers. "Thank you," she said.

"I'm glad you like this place."

"That too. But really for coming into my life and showing me what it's like to really be loved. Thank you."

Dinner meandered for well over an hour and several courses till Correk finally asked Vernon to stop. "We have somewhere else we need to be, but we'll come back another time."

Correk paid the bill despite all Vernon's protests and the couple made their way out of the restaurant, occasionally stopped by someone wanting to introduce themselves to the Fixer. They finally reached the sidewalk and Leira took in a deep breath of fresh air. "I kind of get why Turner uses that trick to just pop in and out of places. Exits as the Fixer are not easy."

"I ate too much."

"Ixnay on the acksnays on the way home, I take it."

"I'll walk it off. We'll see."

"That's the way to muscle through. Where are we walking to this time? No, that's okay," said Leira, holding up her hand. "I can walk this time."

"We take a turn at the end of this street and head up the hill into the Willen's part of town.

"We're off to see a Willen, the wonderful Willen of Oz," sang Leira as they came to the end of the block and turned left, heading up the street where the light grew dimmer. Gradually the state of the cottages they were passing grew shabbier and potholes appeared in the street. They kept climbing, trudging up the hill till they got to the corner of Mayfield and Laurel and Correk pointed to the left. They walked down the narrow street as Willen faces appeared at the windows, one by one, pulling their curtains shut till they got to the next house and the next faces appeared.

"They all know we're here." Leira let herself relax and slipped back into bounty hunter mode, scanning the area.

"That's usually the case in this part of town," said Correk. "Willens have reason to fear magicals and humans, and they're very protective of each other. There's always a relay system passing information or just good gossip. But tonight, they are probably making sure we are the only magicals passing through here."

"It's like an added layer of protection."

"If there was a problem, they would turn off the lights in their windows and we would know to turn around and leave. No questions asked. Turner taught me that one."

Leira looked up at the warm glow from different windows. "So far, so good."

Correk counted the houses from the corner and picked

his way through the trash on a lawn, walking around to the back. Leira was right behind him. She was still looking everywhere for anything that seemed out of place in a part of town where that was the norm. Correk stepped up to the back door of a blue cottage and rapped on the door, waiting. A dingy yellow gingham curtain was pulled back and two grey eyes stared straight at Correk. The curtain fell back into place as lock after lock could be heard twisting and turning, bolts sliding out of place. At last, the door opened and a round elderly Willen wearing a blue button down shirt with a torn pocket and shiny cuffs at the sleeve hurriedly waved to them to step inside. He gave a last look to the left and the right before shutting the door behind them.

"Were you followed?" he asked, his whiskers twitching.

"Not that we noticed," said Leira.

The whiskers twitched again. "Not very reassuring Jasper Elf."

"Leira, you can call me Leira."

"I go by Barnum but keep that to yourself. The network of Willens is to be kept a secret. Who you see here, what you hear here, just forget about it."

"Consider it done. Do you have the ring?"

The Willen shushed her, waving his paws and scowling. "No need to say what it is. Yes, I have the package." He reached into the folds of his skin, digging around. "Uh huh... uh huh," he said, digging some more. "Uh huh... wait, nope, uh huh... Okay, yeah, got it!" He pulled out the small box and carefully opened it showing Correk the signet ring inside. "Did we do well?"

"You did more than you know." Correk took the box

and shut it, sliding it into his inside pocket. He reached into another pocket and pulled out three gold coins. "For your troubles. A tip."

"Oh, well if you must. I never asked, if anyone asks you. I'm happy to serve."

"Of course," said Correk, handing over the coins, which quickly disappeared into a fold of skin, jingling as they settled into place. "Best be off. Longer you're here, the more trouble we can expect."

"Thank you, Barnum," said Leira, hugging the Willen around his neck.

"Oh well, it's nice to know what they say about you is true," said the Willen, wiggling his whiskers. "You treat Willens with respect, the respect we've always deserved. Word gets around, you know. Okay," he said, opening the back door, "Scoot, off with you. Hurry home and don't stop anywhere. We can keep an eye on you for part of the way but you're on your own once you leave Mayfield. Hurry, hurry." He gently nudged them out the door and shut it with a click, followed by several locks sliding back into place.

"How about we skip stopping for your snacks just this once," said Leira, as they walked down the street, faces appearing at the windows again.

"Good plan. I still have plenty left at home, maybe."

"Thank you for a really good date night."

"Always, Leira, always."

CHAPTER TWENTY-FIVE

Correk was already undressed and sliding under the covers. The endless stream of magic swirled around him. Different Elves, Kilomeas and Wizards were getting themselves into and out of jams without the need for intervention. It was a constant in the background for him these days and he had grown used to their presence.

Leira was curled on her side and he scootched closer to her, forming himself to her curves and slinging an arm across her. He let out a contented sigh, breathing a warm breath against Leira's neck. She smiled in her drowsy sleep and pulled his arm tighter, pressing her cold feet against his legs. He let her do it almost every night.

The magic continued to swirl adding to his sense of comfort knowing all is well.

Until it wasn't.

A strand of magic began to undulate in distress, pulling away from the larger stream. Correk felt the disturbance and lifted his head, holding still to see if it smoothed out again. The ripples grew till he knew it was time to go. He kissed Leira on her ear and eased his arm off her warm body, trying not to wake her.

But she stirred anyway. "Duty calls?" she asked, rolling over in the darkness and reaching out to touch his face.

"It does," he said, sliding into a pair of jeans. "I'll be back as fast as I can. Keep my side of the bed warm." He pulled a shirt over his head and picked up his shoes.

Leira smiled and rolled toward his side, curling up with her head on his pillow. "Done," she whispered, already falling back to sleep.

He waited a moment, watching her sleep before going out into the hallway and padding down the stairs with his shoes in his hand. He passed by the troll's room and heard laughter from Yumfuck and Nibbler as something heavy slid across the floor. Yumfuck could be heard saying, "Perfect, just like that."

Correk shook his head and continued down the stairs. "I can see why Leira wants to know." He slipped into his shoes, tying the laces and straightened up, a ball of light already appearing in his hand. He pulled it apart till a portal opened on thirteenth street, a block away from the Cuban Club in Tampa, Florida. Correk could see the bright lights behind the historic old building and could hear the crowds cheering. He quickly made his way to the wide boulevard of East Palm Avenue, jogging till he got to the side alley where the trash cans were kept.

Behind the club there were lights strung between four tall palm trees and in the center of the square was a wrestling ring. Two wrestlers in masks were circling each other, growling and stomping. The crowd was shouting for their favorites and waving their arms.

The wobbling of the magic had increased as Correk doubled back to a side door and clapped his hands together sharply, disappearing without a trace.

"Whoa," said a man sitting on the curb, waiting for an Uber. "It is really time for me to get home."

Correk reappeared in a dressing room in the basement surprising a large Kilomea in red wrestling boots and black shorts topped off with a white t-shirt. He was grimacing and gritting his teeth as large fangs appeared at the sides of his mouth and disappeared again. Fur crept up his chest, poking out of his t-shirt and withdrew. His glamour was failing him. He sat down on an examining table covered in a faded green sheet.

"You're the Fixer, right? What happened to the old dude?" The Kilomea squeezed his eyes shut and curled his hands into fists, the glamour slipping and coming back. "Shit, never mind. Can you help me?"

Correk put his hand on the Kilomea's shoulder and felt the static in his energy. Something was blocking it. Another spell.

"Name's Rocky. Rocky Acevedo but out there I go by Raging Rocky. Uhhhhh." He doubled over suddenly, the glamour slipping again. This time it took a moment before the glamour came back.

"Who are you wrestling tonight, Rocky? Who's on the card with you?"

"What?" Rocky sat back up, shaking his head to clear it. "Uh, it's Diamond Dragon. He's my nemesis in the ring. Fans love it. He's my neighbor in Bayshore Beautiful, just two doors down. We play poker in my garage all the time but tonight I'm gonna take him down. That's if I can get this fucking magic to work."

"What's Diamond Dragon's real name?"

"Stanley Pickering, why? I don't think he can help me get out of this one. Man, he will never let me forget if I have to forfeit. I suppose I can say it's stomach flu." He grabbed Correk by the front of his shirt, inches from his face. "But I can't go home like this. I'll scare the crap out of my neighbors. My kids live in that neighborhood. My wife will throw me out." He shoved Correk back and forth, pleading for help.

Correk squeezed one eye shut against the onslaught of hot breath that reeked of pizza and beer. He pulled his shirt loose and took a step back. "I don't think that's going to be a problem. I have to go check on something but by the time I get back, your glamour should be back to normal." He was already searching the nearby streams of magic for the one he needed. *Found it.*

"I only have another fifteen minutes."

"That's more than enough time. Stay here, don't let anyone in and do your best to take some deep breaths." Correk had disappeared from the room and reappeared in the dressing room down the hall. Another wrestler was swinging his muscled arms, shiny with sweat and oil. He was dressed in black boots and silver shorts with black leather straps crossing his bare chest. "What the fuck?" He took a swing at Correk, easily missing as Correk ducked out of the way.

The Fixer countered with a string of light with two illuminated balls on either end. He swung it at the wrestler's ankles, wrapping him as they coiled around his legs, pulling tight till he dropped to the floor. Correk came and kneeled on his chest, pressing down. "Hello Stanley. We've never been formally introduced. I'm the new Fixer. And you, Stanley, neighbor to Rocky, are a wizard with some sketchy familial connections."

Stanley grunted and tried to shove Correk off his chest, but Correk kept him pinned. "I'm stronger than I look, Stanley and I know more magic than you can comprehend. If necessary, I can restrain you further. That going to be necessary, Stanley Pickering, or are you ready to listen?"

Stanley stopped struggling at the mention of his last name. "How do you know my name?" he growled.

"Your neighbor, Rocky, who seems to think you two are friends, told me. Now, what would Rocky do if he found out you're actually a part of the dark families? An angry Kilomea is not a pretty sight."

"You won't tell him. You're the Fixer. You help magicals."

"I help magicals who are in trouble. Doesn't mean I can't be the reason they get in trouble." He pressed down harder till Stanley gasped for air. "You, Stanley, are going to remove the spell you put on your good buddy, Rocky and you're going to go out there and have a clean match. If you don't, I'm gonna spill everything. And if you try it ever again, I'll be back, and I'll tell him then. It's a lifetime promise."

"You're too busy to keep watch over me."

"You're right, which makes this even more annoying."

"You don't know what Rocky did to me! He took my riding lawn mower and ruined the alternator but claims he didn't. I need to win tonight to make up for the money I lost from fixing the damn thing."

Correk eased up on Stanley's chest and put his hand on his shoulder, whispering a spell. The pair disappeared, reappearing in Rocky's dressing room.

"What the hell is Stanley doing here? I didn't want him to know!"

"He knew before you did," said Correk. "Tell him. Tell him or I will."

Stanley scowled, shaking his head. "I thought you said we could keep this between us."

"I can see that there's a little more to this and it's going to take some group honesty. Go on, your match starts in a few minutes. If either one of you want to be out there, start."

Stanley hemmed and hawed till Correk nudged him in the back. "I put the spell on you to mess with your glamour."

"What? Rocky jumped off the table, ready to tear into Stanley but Correk stepped between them and looked Rocky in the eye. "Now you tell Stanley what you did to his lawn mower."

Rocky growled, spit bubbling at the corner of his mouth as Correk calmly looked him in the eye. "Fine! That thing was wearing down already. It's not my fault it picked when I was using it to finally fail."

"I had it checked in the spring. It was fine till you borrowed it."

"Rocky, you borrow something, you return it, so it still works. You owe your neighbor a new alternator."

Correk slowly turned toward Stanley making sure

Rocky didn't make any sudden moves. "Stanley, apologize to Rocky for putting a spell on him and remove it at once. Or else."

"Or else what?"

"Or else I'll rip you limb from limb!" yelled Rocky, snorting with anger.

"I'm not afraid of you!" Stanley pulled out a retractable wand from a side pocket on his shorts and unfolded his wand.

"Or else I'll leave you two alone in here," said Correk, rolling his eyes. "Do it Stanley. It's obvious he's your friend and you're still going to be neighbors after tonight. He was wrong, and now you're wrong. Fix it."

Stanley dropped his head and muttered, "Fine." He lifted his chin. "But I want a new alternator."

Correk tilted his head and looked at Rocky, arching an eyebrow.

"Fine, I suppose I may have broken it. I'll Venmo you. Will that do?"

"I can live with that." Stanley lifted his wand and said, "Novis. Restituere." Steam radiated off the Kilomea as the spell burned off and the glamour returned, leaving a muscular, dark haired man.

There was a knock at the door. "We're ready for you, Rocky."

"I gotta get back to my dressing room," said Stanley. "Look, I'm sorry I did that, Rocky. I let my resentment get the best of me. Fair match?" He held out his hand and Rocky hesitated, but he finally took it and shook his friend's hand. "You still coming over to cook out tomorrow?" asked Rocky.

"Okay, I'm taking him back to his dressing room," said Correk, as Stanley nodded his head. The two were gone before Rocky could say anything else. Stanley quickly found himself back in his dressing room and looked around for his mask. "Hey, you're not gonna tell him about my family, are you?"

Correk shook his head. "No, but maybe you should, Stanley. He's your friend and he'll understand and then you won't have to worry about a secret coming out."

There was another knock at the door. "Diamond Dragon, it's now or never. You coming?"

"On my way."

"Good luck to both of you." Correk clapped his hands sharply and was gone. He reappeared back on the street where he had started, quickly opening a portal to his hallway. He stepped through, letting it shut behind him and went up the stairs, passing the troll's room.

"Shhhh... shhhhh," he heard as he passed by.

He chuckled and kept going, taking the rest of the stairs two at a time till he was at his bedroom, already taking off his shirt and unzipping his pants, stepping out of his shoes. He went to his side of the bed and folded back the covers, gently sliding Leira over to make enough room. He lay down next to her as she stirred and curled up next to him, pushing her feet up against his legs. He lay his head down on the pillow and smiled, kissing her head. "I love you," he whispered, as he fell to sleep.

"This meeting is now in session," said Senator Thatcher, knocking the gavel against its stand with a sharp thwack. "Our first order of business will be the sale of Oriceran crops in our marketplace."

Wolfstan Humphrey sat at the far end of the dais, barely able to contain a grin. He was still recovering from his wounds, but his suit covered most of them and a spell was keeping most of the pain at bay. It was worth it all to him, just to have this seat. Every plan has setbacks, he told himself. Trevilsom had taught him that. But in order to survive and conquer, he had to be willing to wade through defeat and crush his enemies. This seat was proof of how right he was in his philosophy. It meant everything to him.

"Mr. Humphrey, do you have anything you want to share?" The Senator from Wyoming was leaning forward in order to see him better.

It's working at last, he thought. "I have a few suggestions."

CHAPTER TWENTY-SIX

L eira rolled over toward her phone, lifting it up to check the time. "Four thirty?" she whispered as the phone continued to buzz. She looked at the number as she slid her thumb across, answering the call.

"Hello?" she said in a hushed voice. She slid out of bed, tucking the covers back around Correk. "Doc, what's happened?" Leira tiptoed out of the room as Correk's hand slid across her pillow.

Doc Leahy cleared his throat. "I apologize for the hour, but this can't wait till daylight. Monsters don't keep regular hours."

"It's okay. I've always had jobs with strange hours and monsters tend to like the dark."

"Well, this time it's idiots making monsters. I've been tracking some cousins in the dark families. They've been popping up on the message boards bragging about some stunt they were planning. It's no one in the inner circle but close enough."

Leira held the phone to her ear as she made her way to

the bathroom where she had started keeping a set of clothes for just these occasions. She balanced the phone under her ear as she pulled on a pair of tight, black slacks, zipping them up.

"They've gotten their hands on a very powerful artifact and are already using it. They've uploaded a video to the web and it's already got a million views in just the past hour. I'm sending it to you now."

Leira lowered the lid on the toilet seat and sat down, pressing the speaker button as the video popped up on her phone. She pressed play and watched a video of a crowded nightclub with different colored lights flashing and the sound booming. A young witch was sticking out her tongue toward the camera, laughing and spinning around. She was holding a wooden jewelry box that fit into the palm of her hand. She put a finger to her lips, grinning and crept up behind a young woman with wavy blonde hair wearing a halter top and jeans. Her back was to the witch as she swayed to the music.

The witch raised her eyebrows, still smiling as she slowly opened the box. Spinning whirligigs, black beetles, flew out of the box, a shroud of dark fog accompanying them. They flew around the girl's head, creating a halo of dark mist, spinning faster and faster. The shroud seeped into the girl's hair, sinking into her skin as she uselessly batted at the beetles.

One by one the beetles came to rest on her head, disappearing into her hair.

Suddenly, her back arched, her shoulder blades drawing closer. She spun around toward the camera, her eyes completely dark. She opened her mouth to say something and the beetles emerged, flying back to the wooden box. The witch waited till they all returned before shutting the lid.

Zombies, mouthed the witch to the camera with the tortured girl behind her. The girl's dark eyes were wide and she was shoving people out of her way as the video ended.

Leira could feel her heart beating faster. "What the fuck did I just watch?"

"An old Egyptian artifact that was thought lost. It creates zombies out of people. The affect is only temporary and lasts a few hours..."

"But a lot can happen in a few hours. Damn." Leira put the phone down on the sink and pulled out a dark blue shirt, buttoning it up the front. She pushed her feet into her sneakers and started tying them. "Where could they have gotten an artifact like that."

"Clearly from some mystery vault owned by the dark families."

Leira thought of Ariana and their family's vault. "I don't believe that Ariana would risk everything on a trick pulled in a nightclub. She's way too ambitious for a move like that."

"Then at the least her security is lax, which considering what they may possess, is even worse. I need you to leave immediately and retrieve that box and protect anyone who's still under the effects. Leave the two wizards and the witch to the Silver Griffins. They'll be right behind you so you have to hurry."

"Why not tell the Silver Griffins to get the artifact?" Leira stood up, checking her teeth in the mirror.

"Their vault has been compromised in the past and there's rumors of a mole in their organization. I have better ways to secure something like that right now. An artifact like that could cause a lot of harm to the way humans see us as well. I'm sending you the coordinates. They're at a popular haunt for magicals in New York City. Bob Dylan used to hang there. So did Jimi Hendrix."

"They were both magicals? Let me guess. Light Elves."

"Both are Wood Elves. There's something to being able to see in so many directions at once. Makes you deep. Let me know as soon as the box is secure. One more thing, Leira. No matter what Ariana may have said to you, it's just a marketing pitch. You cannot trust her, not at all. I know that you've known me only a very short time, but I come from that network of families. I have known that girl her entire life. In some ways she's more dangerous than Sirius because she's smarter and not as petty."

"Warning delivered. I know not to turn my back on her, but I'll also keep in mind that she could be willing to straight up stab me in the chest while looking me in the eye."

Leira hung up the phone and went back to her bedroom to write a note.

"Your turn now?" Correk's face was partially mashed into the pillow and his eyes were half open.

"Seems to be. I have a mission that can't wait. Idiot wizards and a witch playing mean with humans."

"You need me to come with?" he asked, his eyelids floating down.

Leira smiled and leaned across the bed to kiss him on the cheek. "No, I'm good. I'll be back by breakfast." Correk lifted his hand to wave as Leira left the room, checking her phone for the coordinates. Leira stood in the hallway by their bedroom opening a portal. On the other side was Minetta Street in Greenwich Village. She stepped through, pulling the portal closed, sparks whizzing around her feet on the dark pavement. The streetlight overhead was burned out and that part of the street was quiet. In the distance was the sound of a police car making a single, *whomp whomp* noise with their siren. She made her way down the street, turning onto MacDougal and headed for the red and green neon sign of Cafe Wha? halfway down the block. A red velvet rope was set up outside, but no one was manning it anymore and the line was empty.

Young women in short skirts and blousy tops and platform shoes were stumbling out the door as Leira got closer, almost falling into her. She swerved just in time as one of the girls put out her arm to catch herself on the brick wall.

In the opposite direction Leira could see a minivan pulling up and parking a block away under a lone streetlamp. Two middle aged witches were getting out, looking around till they spotted the Cafe Wha? sign. "This is gonna be a close one," muttered Leira, picking up the pace.

Leira went down the stairs toward the club, the music still playing and wove her way through the remaining patrons. A long bar stretched most of the left side of the room and overhead were exposed pipes and beams. Tables and booths filled the center of the room and at the far end was the stage. Just in front of the stage were still dancers bunched up together, dancing with everyone all at once.

Leira spotted the witch from the video right away. She

was jumping up and down in time with the music on the edge of the dance floor. Leira pulled in enough energy to detect the magicals in the room. They were dotted everywhere, outnumbering the humans. Right next to the witch was a short, skinny wizard with a buzz cut on the sides of his head and floppy curls on the top. He was doing a manic takeoff of the twist, biting his lip for effect.

"There's one. Where is the other?" Leira stepped closer and saw between the two another wizard. A taller, pudgier version of the same thing but with darker hair. He was dancing with the temporary zombie girl, twirling her around. Leira felt the energy tickling her feet, wanting to rise up and seek out the three magicals. "No one should lose their ability to choose," muttered Leira. She let the magic slowly rise in her system, setting a careful intention. *Retrieve the box, but quietly.*

A stream of energy flowed up through her left arm and shot out her fingers in the shape of a lizard's tongue, zapping at the box and yanking it from the witch's hands. It easily flew to Leira's outstretched hand, landing softly as she closed her fingers around it.

"Hey!" she shouted, disturbed out of her reverie. "You don't know who you're messing with!" She spun around, her wand out and ready to take on Leira. The two wizards slowly catching on and joining her by her side. But their expressions changed when they saw who they were about to fight. "I know you," said the witch, the color draining from her face. Behind them, the young woman still under the spell continued to lurch around the dance floor, stumbling and falling and picking herself back up again.

The shorter wizard held up his hands, whining, "We

don't want any trouble. It was just a joke. You have the box now. We can leave."

"I'm afraid it's already a little too late for that." Leira glanced back at the stairs and saw the two Silver Griffins making their way into the club, scanning the room. One of them swirled her wand overhead killing the music and raising the lights. The other waved her wand and said in a loud, stern voice, "Never was, never will be." The humans sprinkled throughout the room froze where they were, a drink halfway to someone's lips, a purse almost on someone's shoulder. The girl under the spell stood still in the center of the dance floor, her body still giving off small twitches.

The bartender came out from behind the bar about to protest until he saw the agents and retreated, holding up his hands. "I don't want any trouble. Do what you have to do."

The two agents zipped past Leira as the other magical patrons hurriedly made their way toward the exit and up the stairs. "You have them?" asked one of the agents, tending to the girl still jerking in the middle of the dance floor.

Leira waited just long enough to make sure the agents had grabbed the trio and she quickly headed for the door as well. She heard the young witch exclaim loudly, "I'm telling you, I don't have the artifact. That bitch took it!" But Leira was already at the top of the stairs and quickly emerged onto the street.

She was about to turn and head in the direction she had come when she saw a familiar figure standing in the shadows halfway down the block. "Ariana," she muttered, slipping the box into her pocket. She walked up to the head of the dark families and asked, "What brings you here?"

Ariana was wearing a long, dark trench coat, belted at the waist. "I imagine the same thing that drew you here. Where are they?"

"They're inside the club. The Silver Griffins have them."

Anger flashed in Ariana's eyes. "Did you do that?"

Leira narrowed her gaze. "If I did, it's not your business. But this time I didn't. They managed to draw a lot of attention on their own. It's too late to grab them back," said Leira, starting to walk past Ariana.

"They had better hope the Silver Griffins keep them," hissed Ariana.

"I'm going to assume those three pulled off a heist under your nose. That's not good news. Get your house in order, Ariana. You have too much at stake." Leira turned the corner of the building, not waiting for whatever retort Ariana was about to make and quickly opened a portal, wasting no time stepping through to the hallway near the kitchen, and closing the opening behind her. "That must have stung," whispered Leira. "A fragile truce that's full of holes. We'll see how long it lasts." She gingerly took the box out of her pocket and went into the kitchen, laying it on the counter. She took out her phone and texted Doc Leahy. *It's secure. Meet me in my alley and I'll hand it over. Beware of the wards.*

Her phone quickly pinged. *I'm on my way.*

Leira scooped up the box and opened the back door, pushing the screen door and stepping out onto her porch. She looked up at Angel and Matt's window as a light flickered on and a shadow passed by the window on the other side of the curtain. Leira heard the sparks hitting the gravel and turned to see Doc Leahy striding quickly down the alley, his long coat flying out behind him. "Was there any trouble?"

"Depends on what you mean by trouble," said Leira, stepping just outside the wards and handing over the box. "Ariana was there. Someone must have tipped her off. She was not happy about the Silver Griffins beating her to the hoodlums."

"Did she ask about the artifact?" Doc Leahy slid it into a containment bag and put it in his pocket.

"I didn't give her the chance."

"I have something extra for you." Doc handed her a piece of paper with longitude and latitude on it. "That Light Elf, Wolfstan Humphrey. Some of the darklings on the web have spotted his training camp for mutants." Doc Leahy's expression soured. "He's slipping. You can't get close to it, but you can see it from a nearby peak. Maybe this will help."

"An actual note on paper. The master of the internet is going old school," said Leira looking at the coordinates.

"I'm clever enough to know how easily the internet, even magic, can be pierced. Sometimes a piece of paper is the most secure way to go."

"I know this range. It's in West Texas in the Guadalupe Mountains. Nana took me there when I was young. Thank you for this." Leira looked up at the sun just starting to rise over the building as the sky grew lighter. "You'd better get going before everyone is up and someone locks out their window."

"Your fee is already in your account. I wired it before

we spoke. I'll be talking to you." Doc took off walking down the street and turned at the corner without ever looking back.

Leira wandered back up her steps, suddenly feeling in need of coffee. She pulled the screen door and went inside to find Correk pouring grounds into the coffee maker. "We are perfect together," she said, hugging him from behind.

"Well, yeah. That's obvious. All is well?"

"All is well," said Leira, resting her head on his back.

CHAPTER TWENTY-SEVEN

Perrom crouched next to the peckenberry bushes, picking off the sweet dark berries near the bottom and popping them into his mouth with his right arm. The sounds of the Dark Forest were comforting and familiar to him as birds darted overhead and different animals crawled along the branches. He stopped picking berries and rocked back on his heels, listening intensely. "I know you're there. You may as well come out of hiding."

The large oak tree shook, scattering leaves that drifted down to the forest floor. The Dryad stepped out of the tree, pulling herself away from it.

"I should have known better than to be picking berries near a large oak." Perrom went back to his picking, ignoring his mother.

"You haven't spoken to me in days. I wanted to make sure you were okay without invading your space."

"So, you hung out in a tree watching me eat. It's creepy, even for you."

The Dryad looked around at the forest, letting the

words sink in before she said anything that might accidentally wound an already injured soul. "It's not over. We'll find another way."

Perrom bit down on a berry, an edge to his voice. "The Gardener told me what happened. I know your attempts failed miserably. You might have even made it worse."

"There could still be a…"

"There is no way!" He pressed his eyes closed, a tear hanging off his lashes. "Can you not leave me in peace?"

The Dryad opened her mouth to say something but was distracted by voices traveling in their direction. "Who would travel this deep into the Dark Forest? Fools." She quickly went back to the oak tree and merged with it, receding till all that remained was the tree and Perrom crouching nearby.

Perrom ignored the sounds, staying where he was and doing his best not to think about anything.

A shriek cut through the air along with the sound of breaking branches and someone running. Perrom finally stood and looked through the woods, his irises looking in different directions. The Dryad reemerged from the tree, keeping one hand on the oak, listening for distress from the other trees nearby.

"Someone is hunting and it's not animals they're after. You need to help," said the Dryad.

"This is not my land. Not my problem," said Perrom, turning to go in the other direction.

"Help! Help me!" A female Light Elf cried out, stumbling through the forest. Perrom hesitated, his right hand balled into a fist.

"If you won't help…" The Dryad shut her eyes,

commanding the trees. The message was relayed quickly, passing through the roots till it found the hunter.

Erickson looked down at his feet, surprised to find roots coming out of the ground, growing rapidly around his ankles and feet. But he was beyond caring about anything but his self-designated mission. He wanted revenge and it was all he could see.

Running away from in the Dark Forest was a group of Light Elves and they were about to get away. He was tired of losing and feeling the loss of the Silver Griffins. He wasn't willing to see anything else slip from his grasp. He flicked his wand at the roots. "Hyacinthum flammae!" A blue flame crawled across the roots, turning them to ash as he shook off his boot.

The Dryad cringed in pain, feeling it through the trees, squeezing her eyes shut.

"You won't fucking stop me, you damn haunted forest!" Erickson trudged forward with his wand ready. This time he was going to kill them where they stood. He was done bargaining. It was past due.

"Help them," growled the Dryad, opening her eyes and looking at her son. Perrom's irises all came to rest on his mother's anguished face. His lips curled in turmoil and his artificial hand was clenched in a fist.

"For you," he whispered as he ran past her in the direction of the fight. It didn't take long for Perrom to overtake Erickson. He knew the forest far better and could take shortcuts easily outpacing him. But Erickson was almost on the Light Elves and was already whispering a spell, sure of his victory. So focused, he didn't hear the Wood Elf flanking him on his right side.

Perrom detested the artificial arm but he had also learned a few useful things about it. He summoned a fireball, watching it grow in the mechanical hand, taking on a blue and black hue with different peaks at the top. He hurled it at Erickson, catching him off guard and cutting off the spell. The fireball circled the former Silver Griffins agent, burning as it went, singeing his clothes and blistering his hand till he dropped the wand and screamed out in pain. The flame continued to burn, closing in on the wizard's neck as the Dryad caught up to her son and saw what was happening.

"No…" She whispered a spell, lifting her hands above her head and looking up at the sky.

Rain began to fall on an otherwise clear day, streaming down on their heads and putting out the fire. Erickson fell to the ground, wounded but still alive, his wand charred and smoking. The refugees he had been hunting kept running, making their escape till they could circle back to where they would be met and taken away to Earth.

Perrom looked at his mother and then at Erickson and shook his head. "No one wants justice anymore." He trudged off into the forest, quickly hidden by the dense foliage in search of more berries, doing his best not to think of anything. "Ossonia," he said, only once, before pushing the thought out of his mind.

CHAPTER TWENTY-EIGHT

Leira arrived early to the meeting room and saw that only a few of the senators had arrived. *Something's not right.* A feeling had been bothering her since she came into the room, but she couldn't quite place it. There was a low thrumming across the back of her neck that wouldn't leave.

Senator Rowling from New Hampshire came in the side door reserved for the Senators and took her seat. She glanced to her right anxiously, scowling at the empty chair next to her on the end of the dais. Senator Thatcher came in next, bustling to his seat in the middle behind the wooden name plate that bore his name and the title, *Committee Chairman.* The Senator lifted his gavel without looking at Leira and knocked it against the wooden sound block. "This meeting is now in session," he said brusquely.

Leira narrowed her gaze, looking carefully at each of the Senators. None of them would look to their far right or directly at Leira. They would all make terrible poker players. She pulled in energy through her feet, curling up through her legs causing the vibration across her neck to increase. Her eyes glowed, catching Senator Thatcher off guard, who hammered the gavel three more times. "No magic in the meeting chambers," he bellowed, half out of his chair.

But it was too late.

Leira saw what they were trying to hide. She would know that magical trail anywhere. Wolfstan Humphrey's poisonous glittering trail clung everywhere to the last chair on the right, weaving in and out of the arm rests and sparkling against the back. *Fresh tracks.*

The symbols lit up along Leira's arms, turning over deliberately predicting a dark future. She looked down and read them, her chest moving up and down as her heart beat faster. "Fools," she whispered. She marched toward the dais till she was right under Senator Thatcher's nose. "What have you done? You've let a rabid dog into your world."

"Ms. Berens, step back," ordered the Senator, hitting the sound block over and over. "I will not be talked to that way. We have the right to ask whoever we want to sit on this committee!"

"Sit on the committee?" Leira stepped back, dumbfounded, her eyes growing wider. "You have no idea who you're dealing with or what he wants from you. You think you do. You think you've seen the worst that humans have to offer, but this is a magical who is a monster above all others. You have threatened your very way of life."

Senator Bleeden put his hand over the gavel, pressing down firmly. "We asked Leira Berens to be our first bounty hunter because we trusted her integrity above all other magicals. We knew she would always tell us the truth. If

Ms. Berens is saying we have made a grave mistake, I'd like to know more. So would you."

Senator Thatcher loosened his grip around the handle of the gavel and let it drop. He rubbed his hand on his face and tucked his chin for a moment. He looked up again, directly at Leira. "Do you have proof? We're going to need proof."

"This is something I'm going to have to show you, and it will be all the proof I'll ever need. I'm going to need an assist from someone and a lot of trust from all of you."

Correk stood in the meeting chambers in his long tunic, suede pants and tall boots. His hair was tied back with a leather strip and his bow was strapped to his back along with a quiver of arrows. A dagger in a leather holster was tied at his waist.

The Senators were all eyeing him cautiously. Senator Rowling had changed from her high heels into a pair of blue Keds peeking out from her matching blue slacks.

"I let Doc Leahy know what we were doing. He's standing by with his medical services. You came prepared for a battle too." Leira stood next to him at the far end of the room with her head close to his.

"We're taking very important human beings near Wolfstan Humphrey's biggest secret, which happens to be a monster army training facility. This may not end well."

"Do you think it's a mistake?"

"I think it has to be done. But we have to get them all

back here in one piece as well. Is Jackson meeting us there?"

"Yes, along with Mom and Nana and a few others. We'll be able to surround the Senators and create a barrier just in case. An *in case* I hope we don't have to use."

"Then let's get started. The sooner we start, the sooner Wolfstan is exposed and removed." Correk pulled his hands apart, creating a ball of light.

"Is this theater really necessary?" asked Senator Deane, nervously watching the portal open.

"You're welcome to sit out, if you're not up to it." Senator Bleeden looked at him over his reading glasses, barely hiding his annoyance. He had changed to sneakers and taken off his suit jacket, replacing it with a windbreaker.

The portal grew to reveal the top of Bartlett's Peak. Senator Rowling was the first one through the opening, walking out far enough to get a view of the Ponderosa pine and Douglas fir trees dotting the side of the mountain. To the west were salt flats stretching out for acres. A purple shimmer hovered just above them.

The rest of the Senators quickly followed, stepping through and looking around, their eyes wide. Leira put out an arm for the elderly Senator Thatcher and waited near the portal till Correk came through, shutting it behind him and stamping out the sparks.

"I thought you said we would have protection," said Senator Thatcher, scanning the area.

"Give it a second."

Leira heard the pop of a portal opening and the familiar sounds of friends and family. Eireka came through the rim of trees first with Mara right behind her. "I came as soon as I got your message and brought an ally from the school. Meet Professor Eleanor Hudson, a crackerjack witch."

Tall, thin Professor Hudson came through the treeline, her expression grim behind her black-rimmed glasses and her sleek blonde hair fluttering in the wind. She was wearing her black robes from campus, her wand already in her hand. "Gentlemen," she said with an arched brow.

Other magicals quickly piled out of the woods. Toni marched forward holding onto Jack's hand and behind them were other regulars from the Jackalope. Another portal abruptly opened behind the Senators startling them. They moved closer in a cluster toward Leira as the portal grew wider.

"Hi Dad, glad you could make it," said Leira as Jackson stepped through with Louie, his sword strapped to his back. "I was wondering when someone was going to call me," said Louie, grinning. "Looks like we have ourselves a party."

"Where are the Silver Griffins?" asked Jackson. "This seems like their kind of party."

"Over there," said Leira, pointing to a lower range to the right of the training flats behind a thick stand of trees. Jackson pulled out a small pair of binoculars and held them up. On top of a nearby peak were Silver Griffin agents and standing at the front were Lois and Patsy. He watched Lois zing Patsy with a pea sized fireball and Patsy duck out of the way, the fireball dribbling along the ground.

"Lois says she has a plan just in case that could help relocate the soldiers instead of killing them," said Leira.

"My father thinks we'll be able to help them," said Correk, looking out over the land below.

"They are a kind of innocent," said Jackson, standing next to his daughter. "But what can you do with all of that?"

"There may be hope, yet." Leira patted her father's back, her eyes glowing with energy.

"Where do you want us?" asked Eireka, her eyes glowing, her energy seeking out her daughter and wrapping around her.

"Make a semi-circle around the Senators but leave them room to see what's below. Senators, it's time. Does everyone have their binoculars?" Leira pointed to the flats below and the battalion of magicals marching in lockstep across the open land.

Senator Bleeden raised his binoculars and looked down at the mutant magicals, the sun glinting off the mechanical accessories to their bodies. "What exactly are we looking at? What are they wearing?"

Leira raised the binoculars she had brought with her. "They're not wearing anything. They've had parts of their body involuntarily replaced with a mixture of artifacts and technology. They've been turned into a large and growing secret army that's a mixture of what Earth does best and what Oriceran does best. Technology and magic in one hideous form."

"What do you mean, involuntary?" asked Senator Deane, his expression tense as he lifted the glasses again.

"I mean that they were all kidnapped and mutilated without their permission. Their minds are not their own.

Wolfstan Humphrey has been using his company, Fleeker, as a research facility to create this," said Leira.

Correk grimaced, gripping the edge of his knife. "Wolfstan has bigger plans than you were able to see."

Another portal began to open, and Louie slowly took out his sword, ready to greet the surprise visitors. *Caution*, the sword whispered to him. *Steady*.

Pearson Cowley stepped through the portal, surveying the crowd of people. "There you are, Leira Berens. Doc Leahy sent me. An old enemy and now a friend." Pearson looked down on the flats and across to the Silver Griffins standing on the nearby peak. "I've met Wolfstan Humphrey and it was obvious from the start he was far more dangerous than most of the foes I come up against." He looked at Louie and pursed his lips. "You can save the sword for later, Louie. I'm with the Silver Griffins," he said, pushing up his sleeve to reveal a tattoo of two intertwined S's. "Still working for Leira, I see."

Louie put away the sword, looking Pearson up and down. "You look familiar. You worked with Charlie Monaghan, didn't you?"

"Good memory."

"We're wasting time and drawing attention," said Leira, pointing down to the flats. "Focus on why we're here and stay alert. We're bound to set off some kind of alarm eventually. Take a good look at what you see below and then let's get out of here."

"How do we know that these soldiers belong to Wolfstan Humphrey?" asked one of the Senators.

"Take a look at the black SUV along the side of the road. Look at who's standing by the passenger side door," said Correk, looking through the binoculars at a grinning Wolfstan Humphrey.

"Son of a bitch!" exclaimed Senator Thatcher. "I knew something was wrong." He shook his head. "I should have listened to my gut. I didn't see the harm in listening to him, waiting him out."

"Now we can see the harm spread out below us," said another Senator. "What if he were to do this to humans?"

"I think doing *this* to magicals rates right up there too," snapped Toni.

A murmur picked up over the crowd as the group began to argue with each other.

"Look! Down there!" Louie was at the edge of the summit, pointing down toward the field. Leira lifted her binoculars and saw Wolfstan Humphrey pointing up at them, angrily waving his arms. He had yet to spot the Silver Griffins on his other side. He was yelling orders as the first magical in a column began to open portals.

"They're coming to our location. Open a portal, do it now. Take the Senators back!" Correk pulled his bow off his back and readied an arrow.

Leira hastily opened a portal to the Senate chambers and shoved and pushed the Senators, some of them falling onto the carpeted floor on the other side.

Portals began to open all around them, tearing wider as soldiers down on the field entered a portal there and exited on Bartlett's Peak, ready to fight.

The Silver Griffins saw what was happening and split into two groups. The first came through the trees, to the edge of the hill, already wielding their wands, aimed at the portals. The others rushed the field, led by Lois and Patsy.

They were carrying between them an open old leather suitcase covered in faded stickers from faraway places. Patsy had one handle and Lois had the other as they ran in opposite directions.

The suitcase grew in size, larger and larger, until it stretched the length of the battalion, rushing at them, throwing fireballs at the suitcase and the two witches. Patsy dodged fireballs as agents ran to either side, pushing the remaining soldiers toward the open suitcase. Witches and wizards zinged fireballs and conjured shadows to swirl around the mutant soldiers, confusing them without wounding them. Several witches formed a line, yelling out a spell to make the ground slick with ice underneath the soldiers' feet.

One by one, they stumbled or fell into the open space, disappearing from the battlefield. Finally, Patsy let go of her side and the suitcase retracted, whizzing back toward Lois as it shrunk. Lois held onto her handle, bracing herself. Once the suitcase had returned to normal size, she slammed it shut, clicking the lock.

Wolfstan Humphrey raged from the sidelines. He angrily opened a portal to the summit, stepping out behind the few soldiers who had made it to the top. Senator Thatcher was just stepping through the last portal and took a look back at Wolfstan. "You're done!" the Senator yelled as the portal closed, securing the politicians.

Wolfstan turned ashen. He found himself standing in front of a homemade army of magicals with only a handful of soldiers. He caught sight of Pearson Cowley in the crowd and his rage grew. "I will not lose everything! Finish them," he bellowed.

The soldiers marched forward. They were caught under a spell they couldn't escape.

The magicals did their best to turn them back. Professor Hudson flicked her wand, weaving a metal cloth over a soldier's face, blocking his sight. "Good one," yelled Mara. A fireball whizzed by Jack, burning his arm as Toni pulled him out of the way and the fireball kept going, turning a tree to ash in an instant.

The soldiers marched forward, closing the gap leaving the magicals with fewer choices, unwilling to harm them.

BANG!

Jack covered his ears, squeezing his eyes shut. The sound was followed by a cloud of smoke, separating the two groups.

A sudden gust of wind revealed Turner Underwood holding up his cane and wearing his favorite bowler. Next to him was the old King of Oriceran, brought out of hiding.

"He knows something that may help," said Turner. He gave a nod to Correk and waved his cane, the smoke curling around the remaining soldiers. Both the soldiers and Turner were gone in a flash.

Wolfstan Humphrey found himself staring down the tall, muscular king who was dressed in his old battle gear and itching for a fight. Wolfstan pulled out a knife and ripped it through the air, opening a portal that was unstable at the edges. He leaped through to his office as hands from the world in between reached out from the sides.

Everyone else pulled back, not willing to get close.

The portal closed and the small army of magicals that

had come together found themselves standing around the old King of Oriceran.

"That was kind of anticlimactic," said Louie, putting away his sword.

"That's what we wanted," said Mara, swatting at Louie's head.

"We're going to need that enthusiasm for battle at some point, I fear," said the Professor.

"My liege," said Correk, "Turner said you can help?"

"There is more to the world in between than most realize. Even those who are trapped in its realm. There may be more than one way to defeat Wolfstan Humphrey, but first I need to find Lucius. He knows the rest of the story. The shifters will be key to helping those soldiers."

Ariana carried a crystal glass filled with red wine as she descended the stairs under the family house in Rome.

Underneath were old aqueducts that stretched for miles and had not seen water for more than a century. Spider webs caught in her hair as she passed, batting them away.

She got to a spot with a broken yellow tile and pushed on it, sipping her wine. An opening appeared, sliding to the side with a loud, grinding noise, stirring up dust.

She stepped inside and pulled out her wand, lighting the end to guide her way in the darkness. She passed by old crypts full of dry bones of dead ancestors and came to another door, tapping the handle with her wand.

It gave way as she turned the knob, entering the old vault. It was lined with more shelves, meant for the dead but instead different artifacts long forgotten sat waiting on every shelf.

"A witch should always have a plan B," she said, smiling as she took another sip, admiring the collection. "Just in case things don't go my way. See you soon, Leira Berens."

The story is far from over. Leira's adventure continues in *BATTLE MAGIC*

Get sneak peeks, exclusive giveaways, behind the scenes content, and more. PLUS you'll be notified of special **one day only fan pricing** on new releases.

Sign up today to get free stories.

AUTHOR NOTES - MARTHA CARR

OCTOBER 7, 2020

Halloween is coming and in this very active neighborhood, even in the middle of a pandemic, yes, it's still coming. Hundreds of little people who don't understand what a weird year this is.

Totally understandable given none of us are sure either.

But in this instance, we're the grownups and one of the responsibilities that comes with that is figuring out how to have a holiday from a safe distance.

I feel a little like Linus waiting in a pumpkin patch right about now, but it can be done – and I'm willing to try.

One thing I've learned from losing everything in the Great Recession and overcoming cancer a few times is that memories are shaped by what you choose to stare at – and not exactly because of what's happening – especially for children.

Here's where I would like to take a few pointers from the junior members.

They approach everything like it's brand new and without the filters we've developed and mistakenly come to see as truths instead of individual experiences. They ask themselves in that moment, 'Am I having a good time?' There's very little feedback about how it *should* have been. They don't have a list of shoulds yet.

This is where we come in. We can either point out how it should be if only... and how glorious it was for us in the past, forgetting all the things we didn't actually like about it. Or we can work with what is and stretch ourselves a bit and just celebrate.

Along those lines I've ordered clear gift bags with twist ties from Amazon and plan to be filling those suckers with a lot of candy. I'll put the bowl ten feet away from me and sit in a chair with my iPad and watch something on Netflix.

Granted, I live in Austin, Texas so the sitting outside part is a lot easier but you get the idea. I've even seen some adults have rigged long tubes to drop candy into a waiting basket and decorated them in orange and black. Now see, that's how to make it all memorable.

It's really about knowing the people in our lives, in our communities care about us and want to celebrate with us that make the difference. And if you're a kid, lots of candy, of course. But knowing that someone was willing to go out of their way for you can teach a child, and even an adult that the world is basically kindhearted.

That will also make it easier when that same person is faced with a daring challenge to venture out and build their dreams. They'll go knowing there are great people behind them and feeling relatively assured there will also be new kindhearted people in front of them. A much better kind of *should*.

I actually didn't really learn this one till my fifties and that bout of cancer that was supposed to be terminal. I was never alone and people showed up at my door every day to sit with me or to bring food and there was a constant parade of cards and phone calls. That's what I remember first and best. Not the doctors' appointments or tests or waiting. And during the Great Recession when I ended up in an apartment with a bed and three and a half chairs what I remember are all the people who crowded into my place for Thanksgiving around a table we found in the alley. We got a turkey using my neighbor Matt's coupon from work. It's still one of my favorite memories.

I took all that love and used it to keep writing and somehow ended up just ten years later in my dream house with two dogs asleep by my side. Every day I get to sit down and write about witches and Light Elves and strange apothecaries or mermaid trains.

So, here comes Halloween and Thanksgiving is not far behind. It's going to take some creativity to figure out how to stay connected and how to stay safe and how to be kind. This will be my opportunity to take all that I've been given – not just now – but back then and pay it forward.

May we all look back and marvel at the communities we built during this year and may our children learn the world is really a great place to go and build a dream because there are always kind people waiting to help. More adventures to follow.

AUTHOR NOTES - MICHAEL ANDERLE

OCTOBER 9, 2020

Thank you for not only reading this story, but back here to the author notes as well!

You know, I get to read Martha's author notes before creating mine. Not because I'm somehow special, but rather she is usually finished DAYS ahead of schedule and I'm usually finished minutes ahead of schedule.

Occasionally, it works out in my favor.

Like right now. I just read Martha's author notes and I am thinking to myself 'what have I got that goes beyond that?!' I even asked my team if I could just do notes that said:

"What she said!"

I would be allowed but I'm fairly sure they would be shaking their heads in my general direction.

Since I can't add much to Martha's rock-solid emotional author note – I'm going for scientifically eerie.

Like, audio type science.

Did you know that you can make a person feel different

(usually in a negative way) due to a deep infrasonic sound? This is also known as the 'fear frequency.'

Now, infrasound is below the audible human hearing but can still affect us on some level due to the vibrations it creates. The frequency (about 18.9hz) doesn't cause everyone who is around it the same sensations. However, it does cause enough people that experience it to have effects. Not all of them the same.

Some people, for example, get nauseous.

All I know is adding that ability (if it can be safe) would be an interesting way to upgrade YOUR house on Halloween night.

Scary from a distance – That's Infrasound.

Ad Aeternitatem,
Michael Anderle

For Hire: Teachers for special school in Virginia countryside.

Must be able to handle teenagers with special abilities.

Cannot be afraid to discipline werewolves, wizards, elves and other assorted hormonal teens.

Apply at the School of Necessary Magic.

THE MAGIC COMPASS

If smart phones and GPS rule the world - why am I hunting a magic compass to save the planet?

Austin Detective Maggie Parker has seen some weird things in her day, but finding a surly gnome rooting through her garage beats all.

Her world is about to be turned upside down in a frantic search for 4 Elementals.

Each one has an artifact that can keep the Earth humming along, but they need her to unite them first.

Unless the forces against her get there first.

<u>**AVAILABLE ON AMAZON AND IN KINDLE UNLIMITED!**</u>

OTHER SERIES IN THE ORICERAN UNIVERSE

JOIN THE ORICERAN UNIVERSE FAN GROUP ON FACEBOOK!

BOOKS BY MICHAEL ANDERLE

For a complete list of books by Michael Anderle, please visit:

www.lmbpn.com/ma-books/

CONNECT WITH THE AUTHORS

Martha Carr Social
Website:
http://www.marthacarr.com
Facebook:
https://www.facebook.com/groups/MarthaCarrFans/

Michael Anderle Social
Website:
http://www.lmbpn.com
Email List:
http://lmbpn.com/email/
Facebook
https://www.facebook.com/LMBPNPublishing